Hunting the Moon

A novel

Becca Boucher

Write More Publications
Kissimmee, FL

Becca Boucher

This book is dedicated to everyone who believes

that there is something else out there.

Never stop believing in the magic around you ...

Contents

Becca Boucher

Contents (con't.)

"Before we ask if God exists,
we should ask if man really
landed on the moon."
—Sukasah Syahdan

After this I looked and there before me was a door,
standing open in Heaven.
And the voice I had first heard speaking to me
like a trumpet said,
"Come up here and I will show you
what must take place after this."
—Revelations 4:1

Becca Boucher

Prologue

Daemon

I watched her as she made her way into the clearing and slowed, it was almost as if she had forgotten what we were doing here. She looked up at the pink and purple sunset and stopped … a funny time to be having a moment. I was mystified as she bent down, ran her hands through the wet grass and pressed them to her face, still oblivious to my presence on the other side of the clearing. I was supposed to be back by the entrance, the intricately carved gates, but I was afraid to leave her alone. Then, she knelt down and crossed herself. We didn't know if it would help, but it certainly wouldn't hurt. In the last week she spent a lot of the time when she thought she was alone praying for strength … or a miracle … but as I know well, miracles are hard to come by. I got mine when I met her. I would have prayed with her, but, like this meeting, it was something she felt she was supposed to do alone. I watched as she wiped at the tears sliding down her face, but what she did next surprised me … me, who never was surprised. She stood up, stepped further into the clearing and seemed to look straight at me. Then, she started to yell, trying to get his attention instead of waiting for the moon. "Aaron, here I am! I'm tired of this! If you want me so badly, then come and get me! I know you can hear me." Then, she whispered, "You won, you bastard." I lowered my gun and stepped out of the brush, into her line of sight. That's when he shot me.

Chapter 1

Lilly

What had that dream been, anyway? The misty field and the tree line, always out of my reach. I woke in a cold sweat as usual, scared and shaking. It had been the same dream for the entire year since Aaron died. I shook my head and looked at the alarm clock. I sure as hell wasn't going to make it to work today. I rolled over and cried into my pillow. Self pity was something I was getting good at.

I couldn't help but ponder the dream. It was always the same large, empty clearing bordered by woods. The same mist covered everything, thick enough to touch. And, most unnerving, were the eyes that stared at me from the dark woods ... eyes that penetrated my soul and chilled me to the bone. They weren't human in the strict sense, but they were female and hungry. I never told anyone about the eyes. They were the part that caused me to wake in cold sweats, sitting bolt upright, seeming so real.

I looked over at the nightstand and my phone was blinking a message. My stomach turned when I picked it up and saw that it was Nick, my boss. He wasn't happy that I called in sick for work. I picked up the phone and called him back.

"It's the third time this month, Lilly," he said. "If you don't want your job, then surely there's someone out there that does."

It was the same song and dance as last time. He never fired me, they depended on me too much. I mean, who else in that whole kitchen knew what was going on? Could work every position, and would come in at any hour? Well, maybe a tiny part of me worried. "I'm scheduled to work a double this weekend," I replied. That would make it up to him. Plus, all those decisions had to go through Kat.

"Well … just make sure that you're here," Nick replied, then added, "And don't be late!"

I hung up the phone and placed it back onto the nightstand. Pushing up out of bed and shutting my eyes to the blinding sunlight in my room, I made it to the door and into the hall. Staggering to the stairs, my mind was focused on one thing … coffee.

The kitchen was even brighter, why did the sun have to be so cherry? Didn't it know that some people were depressed?

I turned on the coffee pot, sat at the kitchen table and laid my head on my arms, drifting back to sleep. About the time I realized my coffee was ready, the phone rang. I poured a cup and looked across the room to the phone.

Did I want to answer it? The depression was back, making it hard to move, to think, to want to do anything. I was so tired. By the tenth ring, I decided that whoever was on the other end wasn't giving up. As soon as my mother spoke I rolled my eyes, regretting picking it up even more.

"Lilly, are you okay? I was worried when I didn't see your car in the parking lot at the nursing home," she said in a worried tone. "The last time we talked, you sounded out of it. Is everything okay?"

So much for hello. "Well Mom, if you let me get a word in edgewise, I overslept."

She forced out a half-hearted laughed, undeterred. "Have you taken your meds? Anti depressants are very important, you don't want to …"

"Mom!" I cut her off in mid sentence. "I'm fine, just tired. Don't worry. If anything's wrong, you'll be the first to know. I promise." The line remained silent for a tense second.

When she spoke, her voice was strained. "With Aaron being gone a year this weekend, I was afraid."

My turn for silence. "Really, I'm fine. Mom, I'm not in the mood to talk about this right now. I'm late for an appointment. Love you! Got to go!" I hung up before she could protest, then dumped my cold coffee down the drain and crawled back up the stairs to my bed.

Were his arms really around me? I leaned into him, feeling his strong chest push up against me. The scent of his hair … the way it smelled fresh from the shower … wafted toward me. His heart thumped quietly within his chest, vibrating his body. I turned to face him and pull his lips to mine. I had so many questions. Did it hurt? Are you back to stay? What's on the other side? I slowly started to wake and a moment later, he was gone. I pressed my head into the damp pillow and sobbed.

I wasn't sure what woke me this time. The bang? Had it come from the screen door? I thought I pulled the latch tight. Suddenly, the sound of clanking metal on metal woke me up further. It was just a train. The train traffic had increased tenfold on the tracks that ran behind my house in the last year. They were more prolific at night. Night? What time was it, anyway? Rolling over to look at the clock, I was startled to find that it was eight o'clock. I had slept the whole day away. Shit. Some part of me decided to get up, but strangely, I was hungry. I was never hungry any more.

I slid out of bed and rambled to the stairs, turning on lights as I went. Food seemed like a good idea. The old Victorian house hadn't seemed so big when Aaron was here. It was only two bedrooms, two bedrooms that screamed "you are alone" to me now. The thought made me sick to my stomach. Two lives on my soul.

I turned on more lights on my way to the small kitchen and checked the answering machine. The red light blinked … it better be someone good. "Lilly, it's Kat. Tomorrow at sunrise … you … me … jogging. Come on you know you want to. I know you're not at work! If you don't call me back, I'm come over there and break into your house! Call me!"

Kat … the sister I always wanted and never had. She had been my rock over the last year. She held me while I cried and made all the arrangements for Aaron's funeral. Sometimes, she would just be there so I wasn't alone. But at the same time she had changed.

Since we met in college, we had been inseparable. Kat was an only child to divorced parents. Her Mom was dead, and her Dad was long out of the picture, so my family and I had given her the stability she craved. She had dated Aaron first after we all met at a frat party. While they burned things up in the bedroom, Kat's fierce independent nature was too much for Aaron. He wanted someone who would focus only on him and, at the time, I was content to sit back and let him lead the show. Unfortunately, it was a fact that, if I told myself the truth, strained our marriage toward the end. Kat went on to marry a lawyer and used her drive to rise to the top of her profession.

We work together now, in the department that she oversees, a fact that had never bothered me till right around the time Aaron died.

I started to notice things, pushing them to the back of my mind in an order to make Aaron's life easy. The more time I spent in my self-imposed isolation this last year, the more I realized that I was always playing second fiddle to Kat, but she was all I had and making friends doesn't come easy to me.

The same time I reached for the phone to call her back, her knock sounded on the door. "I told you I would come break in," Kat's singsong voice called from the porch.

Forcing a smile, I pulled open the door.

"But isn't this better to have me greet you at the door?" she asked, giving me a big hug as she walked past me into the kitchen. "What are we eating for dinner? I see the salad spinner is ready to go." It was just like Kat to make herself at home. "I'll eat whatever you make me, hon." A bottle of Merlot later, we ate dinner while she peppered me with questions on where I've been hiding. I told her about the dream, leaving out the part about the eyes.

Then, against my better judgment, I tell her what I really want to say. "Kat, I feel like I'm going crazy. Aron's death was my fault," I said as silent tears slid down my face. The remorse and fear running through my body have nothing against the guilt.

Kat sets her glass down so deliberate and slow, I know whatever she is going to say is serious. "Aaron was murdered, Lilly! You didn't pull that trigger. You didn't speed away from a cop and run into that guy crossing the street. You were home ... here ... like you always were."

Was that a jab? Slowly tracing the lines on the table and choosing my words carefully, I set my wine glass down with shaking hands, watching the Merlot slosh against the side. With tear filled eyes, my words come out as a whisper, "I sent him out to the store that night. What was I thinking? It was so late and cold ..."

"Oh, Lilly," she said with outstretched arms.

The next thing I knew I was in Kat's arms. Not knowing if it was the wine or the depression, every thought I ever had about that night but never voiced spilled from my mouth. "We had a fight that night. I don't even remember what it was about, probably something petty and stupid. We were going to have a dinner party with his boss and I threw the bottle of wine at him and it broke. So I made a big fuss, saying that we had to have another one and I sent him out to the package store. I didn't even say goodbye or I love you. That's the worse part, really."

Worry was all over Kat's face as I pull away from her embrace.

Unable to look into her eyes, I crossed the room to the window, stared out into the dark and continued, "When the hospital called they said it had been an accident. But when I got there the police were waiting for me, telling me to call the family, but no one would give me a straight answer. Until that cop from college ... remember Betty Dungin? Anyway, she held my hand and told me that Aaron was shot and had died right there on the fricken sidewalk, Kat!" The face reflected back at me from the dark window contorted with pain. "And all I could think of was that I threw that stupid bottle of wine at him, and for what? Because he was preoccupied with his boss? Because I was feeling underappreciated? I never got a chance to tell him that I love him, Kat! And if he hadn't walked into that store and saw the guy, the kid in the crosswalk would have never been hit, either. Two people died because of my selfishness, Kat!" My head fell into my hands and sobs choked their way out of my dry mouth. "I miss him so much."

I am slightly aware of Kat's reflection in the window as she comes up behind me. She placed her hands gently on my shoulders and turned me to face her. "Why did you wait so long to tell me this?" She asked as she brushed a tear from my cheek. "Do you actually think that it was your fault? Your putting the focus on you when that son of a bitch was hell bent on getting away and it had nothing to do with you! Aaron made the choice to try and stop him; no one made him. That's how Aaron was." Kat's grip on my upper arms tightened. "Look at me, Lilly. I understand how bad you feel, but everyone fights. Aaron knew that you loved him, and I believe that he knows it now. You'll go on, and you will heal. I'm the one left standing there with no one offering me condolences. I lost my best friend that night, or did you forget that?" She actually stifled a laugh. "The only thing your guilty of is a giant pity party. Do you know that whole rationale doesn't even make sense?" I look into the eyes of my best friend and try to smile, but something about this exchange doesn't sit right with me.

After we finish the dishes and Kat left for the night, I made my way to the porch swing with the remainder of the Merlot and a glass. I sit and look at the night sky; it has to be about midnight. Somewhere down the tracks the train whistle blows, a lonesome sound, and the wine warms me. I think. I think of how Kat seemed resentful and secretive, and how much I miss Aaron. But do I miss him or the idea of having someone to take care of? If I truly believed in the teachings from my youth, then he's somewhere in Heaven waiting for me. He's watching over me and helping me, which is a lot more comforting than the thought of an empty void. I chuckle at the thought of a long ago memory, of the two of us sitting on the swing debating the exact same thing.

Aaron had no patience for religion. He was a man of science. If you couldn't prove it with a complex theory, then he wanted no part of it. Well, I bet he's sorry now ... sitting there eating crow as the angels fly around him! The thought crosses my mind that I have had way too much wine. I actually find myself smiling. Then, I heard something coming from the direction of the driveway. The soft sound of sneakers on pavement and the rustle of a coat rushes to my ears. Looking over the porch rail, I saw nothing. I shook my head in disbelief; now I was hearing things. Yeah, I've had way too much wine for one night. I picked up my glass and made my way into the house, lock up, and fell asleep on the couch.

Chapter 2

Daemon

"*Kevin?*" *I looked over at my roommate* as he sat and played with his breakfast. "Have you ever been in love with an older woman?"

He looked up at me. "How much older? Like Betty White older or like cougar older?"

I chucked a fork from the overfilled sink at him. "Like a couple of years older. Okay, maybe five ... but she's more than beautiful."

Kevin chuckled and ran a hand through his wet hair before responding. "Who is she?"

I knew my next answer would put me on his radar as slightly insane, which was not far from the truth. "Well ... Lilly Lawson. I followed her home from work a few times."

Kevin looked at me and rolled his eyes. "*The* Lilly Lawson? As in your-brother-took-out-her-husband Lilly Lawson? You're insane, my friend. Did you know that?" He took a bite of cereal, shaking his head. "Maybe you should even go to confession ... or better yet ... the loony bin."

"Asshole," I mumbled under my breath and turned my attention to the fridge. The truth is, I had followed her home from work only once or twice. And yesterday, when her car wasn't in the parking lot of the nursing home we both work at, I went by her house to check on her when I got off my shift. I even sat in the bushes and watched her drink wine as she sat on her front porch swing. Suddenly, it hit me that I was becoming a stalker. But, after her husband was killed, I felt kind of protective of her. I don't know why I had some strange feeling of responsibility. If the truth was told, I was also drawn to her shoulder-length brown hair that looked messed up in the wind as she walked across the parking lot each morning at work, and her green eyes when she smiled sadly at me in the elevator, but mostly, I was drawn to how kind she was to everyone she met. Every patient and resident in the place loved her. I secretly wondered if she was really that nice or if it was just an act; she had to have an angle. Come on, everybody does.

The sound of Kevin's voice made me snap my head up and hit it on the fridge door. "What the hell did you say?" I asked.

He threw the newspaper at me. "I said, your brother's sentencing is next week. Are you going? It's front page news, dude. He should be damn happy this state doesn't have the death penalty or he'd be a crispy critter, my friend!"

I kicked the newspaper from under my feet and slammed the door shut. "I haven't decided yet. Why should I? Everyone in this hellhole of a town thinks our family is nuts anyway. Maybe if I stay away I can finally separate myself from them."

Kevin was silent for a brief second. "Why did you come back, man? You could have stayed in Boston and no one would have blamed you. I mean, I'm glad you're here, but your mom has no clue who you are anymore, Matty is looking at life in prison, and your dad is long gone."

I took a deep breath, looking at nothing in particular. The truth was that I had no idea why I came back. I took the nursing job here for less money than I was making at MA General in Boston just to work where my mom was; Alzheimer's had taken everything from her. And what was left of the money Matty had already blown on coke and beer, until he killed that guy in the parking lot and the kid crossing the street. "I guess I had to prove that some of us were better," I answered, "and to take care of my mother. No one took care of her when we were growing up. I need to."

Kevin shook his head. "You don't always have to save the day, man," he said. We were quiet as his words hung heavy in the air. He was the first one to break the silence. "Hey, want to go hunting this weekend? It's been ages since we've been. My father has that property up off Rt.2, lots of deer blinds." Kevin's enthusiasm was catchy. Time in the woods might help. "If you can stop the stalking shit for I while that is," Kevin added, ducking as I threw the box of cereal from the counter at him and walked out the door.

"I will be there," I yelled over my shoulder. "You bring the guns and I'll bring the beer … and pick that cereal up!" I left for work with Kevin swearing at the back door.

Chapter 3

Lilly

As I stood on the tracks, I could feel the rumble of the rails under my feet and see the light of the train in the distance. I couldn't move. It wasn't fear that held me to the tracks. It was Aaron. When I stood here I could see him, feel him and hear him. "Lilly, you have to move! The train is coming!" he shouted, but all I could see was his beautiful face. The moon shone down around us, making his hair glow.

"Aaron? Don't leave me yet. I need you!" I begged.

His fingers touched my face and his breath was light on my neck. "I'm here, Lilly, but get off the tracks! The train's coming!" He grabbed my hand.

"Why did you come back?" I asked, stepping off the rails just as the train blew past.

"To warn you," he replied. "Someone is going to try and take you from me."

My pulse quickened. "Who, Aaron?" I felt his hand slipping away and the pain was more than I could bare. "*NO!* Aaron, who? Don't leave me!"

I woke with a start. The alarm was blaring and music filled the room. The sheets were soaked with sweat and tangled around me. Was it real? I looked down at my nightgown and my bare feet and there was no sign of dirt or rocks. *Aaron!* I tried to shake the dream from my mind and focus. Why was I getting up this early? The sentencing! The sentencing was today. I had to get up, to drive to the city. Time. I looked at the clock, 7 a.m. *Shit!* Kat was meeting me at the courthouse at 8:30. I had barely enough time to get up and shower.

Kat didn't want me to go and I had spent half the night wondering why. I had to, to look that son of a bitch in the eyes and watch him be taken away ... for Aaron ... for the boy. I made my way to the bathroom and showered in the dark, trying to push the dream from my mind. I got dressed, choosing my clothes carefully: a lilac button down shirt—Aaron always loved me in purple—a calf-length black skirt, high heels, makeup applied with precision. I was representing Aaron today. I tool one final look in the mirror. "You can do this, Lilly. Be strong," I said to the woman in the mirror strong with resolve, no longer the girl who had skipped down the aisle dressed in white. I smiled. Smiling was getting easier again.

In the driveway I walked past my Volvo with no conscious thought on my part and went to the garage. There it sat. Aaron's Camaro had been parked there since the night my Dad drove it home from the police station. It was Aaron's pride and joy. All red and black with gleaming silver chrome. I opened the door and sat on the soft leather, closing my eyes and taking in the memories, almost feeling Aaron next to me.

"Go on baby, put her in drive. Feel the power," Aaron had said, not yet a year ago. My mind whirled at the memory.

"No way!" I exclaimed in disbelief. "You're really going to let me drive your baby? This car is your life!"

The look in Aaron's eyes grew intense. "No, Lilly, you are my life."

With a sigh, I pushed the memory from my mind and slid the key into the ignition. Suddenly, the car came to life, and with it, a piece of me that had been long forgotten. Here goes nothing.

As I pulled into the parking lot of the courthouse, I wasn't ready for the crowds and news crews that were waiting for me. Bracing myself to face what lay ahead, I made my way through the throng of people in the parking lot.

Kat and the DA were waiting to push me through the crowd and away from the cameramen. Kat leaned into me and said, "Aaron's car. Nice touch."

My insides bristled at her tone. "I needed a piece of him with me." I barely managed to get it out in a whisper. My resolve was starting to waver. We were ushered into the main courtroom and were seated in front of the boys' family. His mother was crying. I stopped and gave her a hug and she gripped my hand. It all seemed surreal, as if I was starring in a TV crime drama.

The noise in the room suddenly stopped as the judge walked in. We stood, the court was called to order, and then the monster was brought in. Matthew Spencer, 26, murderer. It was then that I noticed someone on the other side of the room sitting alone toward the back. He was staring at me.

Grabbing Kat's arm, I shook it to get her attention. "Who's that? He looks kind of familiar. Wait a minute … I think he works with me at High Meadow." My stomach lurched. "Why would he be here?"

Kat followed my gaze and replied, "That, my friend, is the accused man's … well … the bastard killer … that's his brother."

I had to sit.

Chapter 4

It all went by in a blur. The charges were read, the jury roll called, and the victim witness statements were presented. Those were the worse. I nearly lost it when the boy's mother read hers. Cody was so young ... a high school senior who had no idea what hit him. They had to lead her from the courtroom before she was finished. I had to look away. Then Kat, bless her soul, stood up to read my letter for me. It had taken me a month to write. The more I wrote, the more the nightmares had come. There was no way I could read it. I sat in the courtroom staring at him with tears streaming down my face as Kat read. My words were of unfinished dreams, babies never conceived, and my apology never delivered. Kat added her own words at the end as tears streamed from her eyes.

And his killer never looked at me. Never said a word. His shackled hands just rested on the table, unmoving. It took all of my power not to jump up and strangle him with my own hands. I also felt the stare of his brother, and it was not only directed at me. I took a look once to find him staring at his brother with utter hatred. They asked him if he wanted to speak and he rose. "I have nothing to say to the court, your honor. Damn him to hell." He turned and left the courtroom, letting the door slam behind him. One reporter followed.

Then came the words that I had been waiting to hear for a year. "Will the accused, Matthew J Spencer, please rise?" the bailiff asked. He and his attorney complied.

"A jury of your peers has found you guilty of murder in the first degree and has handed down the recommendation for your sentence and I agree," the judge announced. "You are herby sentenced to two consecutive life terms without the possibility of parole for the murders of Aaron Lawson and Cody White. Do you have anything to say to this court?"

All eyes turned to him. "No, your honor, nothing that matters."

The judge stared at him silently. "Well, you are hereby committed to the custody of the court to serve out your sentence at MCI Concord starting immediately. May God have mercy on your soul," the judge said, slamming his gavel onto his desk before him, causing me to jump.

I was ushered through the crush of people out of the court room with a string of "No comment!" Alone in the parking lot, the silence of the Camaro felt like Heaven. I had refused Kat's invitation to lunch and, thankfully, she let me go without a fight, but not before she extracted a promise that I would go straight home.

I started the engine with the windows down. I turned on the radio and Cold Play blared from the speakers. I flew through the back roads out of the city. Right over the city line, I really let her go. As I pressed the accelerator to the floor, the car rumble to life beneath me, thankful to be pushed to the limit just like she was built to do.

Suddenly, I could see Aaron sitting beside me in my memory. "Lilly, do you really think you should be going eighty? Damn! I never knew you could drive like this!"

My grin spread from ear to ear across my face. "You want me to go faster?" I teased as I shifted the car into fourth gear.

Aaron grimaced. "I think I want to see Tuesday," he had joked.

I laughed at the memory. "Aaron, he won't hurt anyone else. He's gone now. *GONE!*" I screamed at the top of my lungs. "I love you, Aaron! I'll never forget you. We won baby, we won!" Tears mingled with my laughter as my foot pushed down harder on the accelerator.

Taking a deep breath, I was behind the airport where the road got curvy when I decided to slow down, although a part of me wanted to let it rip and end it all. At a more reasonable speed of sixty, I looked around at the fall afternoon and the fields. It was then that I noticed it ... the black Chevy truck. I had seen it pull out of the courthouse parking lot into line behind me, but had thought nothing of it. As I slowed it got closer. Too close. I could see the driver in the rear view mirror. "It's him! His freaking brother!" Another look confirmed my suspicions and I pulled over to let him pass, but he pulled up behind me. "What the hell? Okay, Lilly, now you're talking to yourself." He sat and watched me. "Should I get out? All right, Lilly, stop talking to yourself and think about this. What could he want?" Against my better judgment, I opened the door to find him standing by my car. I took a quick step back, trying to find my voice. "Why the hell are you following me!" I demanded.

Chapter 5

Daemon

"*I wasn't following you.* Well, if I was, I didn't mean to," I replied, not really knowing what to say. Yeah, this discussion was taking a turn for the worse. I could tell by the set of her mouth that she was totally pissed and didn't believe a word I said. "I mean, someone would have to be a professional to follow you. Do you know how fast you were going back there?"

She walked two steps away from her car and pointed her finger in my chest. "I don't care if you intended to follow me or not!" she yelled. "The fact is that the brother of my husband's murderer was following me! Do you have any idea how bad that looks?"

"Well if you were that concerned, then why the hell did you get out of your car?" I demanded, turning the tables on her.

Her face, her very pretty face, fell as she tried to come up with a sane response to my question. At that moment, I took her in. She was every bit as sophisticated and stylish as the car she stepped out of. She was stunning in black and purple, her green eyes full of fire; the sadness wasn't taking precedence, for once. Her brown hair was pulled back from her face, showcasing the fullness of her cheeks. I had to look away before she noticed that I was staring. "The truth is," I began calmly, "it got a little tough back there and I was worried that you would take it hard. I wanted to make sure that you got home okay." Did that sound reasonable? I was hoping it did, anyway.

She looked down at the pavement a minute, then she lifted her face to look at me as rage filled her eyes. "*YOU* wanted to make sure that I got home okay? Really? Like my husband got home okay to me? Why don't you crawl under whatever rock you and your brother came out from and stay there!" She turned to get back in her car.

"I am nothing like my brother, you know," I said, my voice barely a whisper.

Something made her stop. "Well, Mr. Spencer, you could have fooled me. Following the wife of the man your brother killed tells me that the apple didn't fall far from the tree," she said as hurt filled her beautiful eyes.

I took her hand and she looked down to the ground as her breath caught. "My name is not Spencer, it's Daemon Kelly," I said. "I took my mother's name to separate myself from him."

Suddenly, she pulled her hand quickly out of my grip. "Well, whatever your name is, you better leave me alone. The next time I see you stalking me I'm calling the cops!" With that, she slid into her car and pulled out so fast that it took a second for her wheels to grip the road. The gravel and sand flew back, stinging my face.

In retrospect, the whole following her home thing now seemed like a bad idea. When I left the courtroom, I pushed by the reporter and stormed out the door. By the time I got to my truck, I was cursing myself for even going there. I had sat in the courthouse parking lot for another hour to calm down. I mean the asshole never even had the courtesy to look up, to even acknowledge his crime. It was as if we had grown up in two separate houses. I hated him.

I was in the process of hitting the steering wheel and swearing to myself when I saw her being led from the courthouse under police protection. Was she going to drive herself? I watched as she got into the '68 Camaro. Wow! I was impressed! And before I knew it I was pulling out into traffic behind her. Believe me, following her was no easy task. She drove like she was at Talladega. I was starting to worry that I was going to be performing first aid on her after she crashed, when she slowed and I caught up with her. It surprised me when she pulled over. I should have driven right by instead of pulling to a stop behind her.

That's how I found myself standing here, watching the back of her car fade into the distance. I turned around and slammed the door of my truck shut. "Damn it! What are you doing, Daemon? Falling for the widow?" The ringing of my cell caught me off guard.

It was Kevin. "Hey, man, you got to get home. The nursing home called and your mom's not doing well at all … and Melissa called." I just stared out over the back of the runway and watched the sky, saying nothing. "Man, are you there?"

"Yeah, on my way!" I said, then snapped the phone shut.

Melissa was one more complication that I didn't need. Before I left Boston, I had told her that it was over. I had received the divorce papers in the mail yesterday. What more could she possibly want?

By the time I got home and talked to the nurse on duty at work, I was in no mood to talk to Melissa. So, I put that off for another day. My mother had turned unresponsive in the middle of the afternoon. From the way her right side drooped, they thought it was a stroke. By the time I got to the hospital to meet her, the diagnosis had been confirmed. As a nurse, I knew that this was a major setback that she couldn't afford. I signed a DNR and a comfort care form, and tried to listen to all the "positives" the doctor outlined.

She could breathe on her own and her swallowing was intact. The paralysis was limited to the right side of her body. With rehab, she could regain some movement, but with Alzheimer's it was hard to get a handle on how much more cognitive function that she had lost. I walked out mid sentence, leaving the doctor staring after me.

"Mr. Kelly, I don't think I was done with this discussion," he yelled after me.

I stopped, but didn't bother to turn around before I answered, "I'm done, doctor. You can't tell me anything else that I don't already know. I'll be back in the morning." With that, I walked to the parking lot and, for the second time that day, I punched the side of my truck. I couldn't think of anywhere that I wanted to go … except to her. What would she think if I showed up in her driveway? Would the police be far behind? Driving aimlessly, I settled for the turn to Fosters' mountain and pulled up to the trail, grabbed the bottle from under my seat and started to walk.

Chapter 6

Lilly

"And you didn't call the police because?" I shifted the phone to my other ear and lay back on the couch, trying to come up with a answer that would make sense to Kat.

"Because, there was something in his eyes that told me he was concerned ... genuinely concerned. I mean, it's creepy, but I don't think he was out to hurt me," I said.

Kat seemed to be screaming into the phone. "What if he shows up at your house in the dead of night? I'm glad that you had a feeling, but it's wrong, Lilly. Deranged stalker, wrong!"

I was silent for a long moment. I didn't know why, but I knew that he would be back, and a part of me didn't really know how I felt about it. Part of me liked the attention and part of me wanted to kill him. I must really be losing it to like attention from the brother of my husband's killer.

Suddenly, the sound of Kat's voice from the other end of the phone snapped me back. "I just worry about you, Lilly. Sometimes you just seem off ... like ... I can't explain it. Like you're far away."

I chuckled. "So, have you and my mom been comparing notes? Setting up doctors for me? I'm okay, Kat ... really. You'll be the first to know if I am loosing it or if a deranged stalker is at my door. Now, go put your kids to bed! I'm fine."

Her voice lost some of its edge. "Okay, Lil, but I'm calling you first thing in the morning. Lock your door and sleep with your phone on your pillow."

My voice held its own taint of venom when I answered her. "Good night, Kat." My mind worked overtime trying to convince me that I was fine. I wish I believed it.

"Lilly … Lilly," a far off, masculine voice called to me. "Come to the window, Lilly." I got up and crossed my bedroom floor to the window. The moon was full and bright, bathing the backyard in soft blue light from some unseen lamp. "Come on, Lilly! Come out back and meet me. The train is coming. The moon is so bright. You should see it." Aaron? Yes, the voice was Aaron's. I got up and ran down the stairs and into the yard. The moon bathed me in the same bluish light as the yard. I followed the path through the trees and out to the train tracks … and I saw him, standing in the night. He reached for my hand, "Isn't it beautiful, Lilly, out here under the moon?"

I reached out to him and asked, "Aaron? Are you real?"

His blond hair glowed with the reflection of the moon. His skin was pale and glorious. His clothes were all white, a perfect balance with the night. He was here! I took his hand, finding it translucent and cold in mine, but it was Aaron, so beautiful that it hurt.

"Oh how I missed you!" I said as silent tears slid down my face.

He smiled, gently touching my cheek. "You can always find me under the moon. Remember how we used to lie on the grass and look up at it, wondering where are future would lead us? I touched it, Lilly! And here I am." I leaned my head on his chest.

"Are you real?" I asked.

He didn't answer me, but held me as he looked up at the moon. "Be careful, Lilly. I don't want to lose you. You need to stay here with me."

I pulled back to look at him, but he faded … like the moonlight behind a cloud. "What do you mean, Aaron?" I asked, but he was gone, leaving wisps of steam off the track in his place. I crumpled to the ground, awash with sorrow and disbelief.

The blaring alarm woke me with a start. This dream was the most vivid yet, even more disturbing than the ones before. I tried to untangle myself from the blankets and noticed that I still had my sweats on from the night before, complete with my sneakers. Had I ever changed for bed? I remembered coming up to shower, but that's all. A cool breeze at my back alerted me to the open window. I looked over and curtains billowed in the October wind. What the hell? I sat up on the side of the bed and put my head in my hands. Sleep walking, seeing ghosts, talking to myself. Whatever it was, I felt like I was losing it. I couldn't admit this to anyone. Who would understand? I crossed myself and said a prayer for sanity. Maybe now that it was over, the sentencing done, this will go away and the dreams will stop. I quickly pushed the thought aside. I had to get ready for work. Give myself more time. I was sure time was all I needed.

Work was the distraction I needed. It was my night to work till six and there was plenty to do. New residents to admit, long term patients to go over food choices with, and outside consults that needed consulting. Before I knew it, five o'clock was upon me and I was making the dinner rounds. When I was up on the long term care floor, I stopped short as I walked into a resident's room. There he was, sitting on a chair in all his glory, holding a patient's hand. The fact that I had remembered him from work when I saw him in the courtroom didn't cross my mind until that second, and the fact that no one had ever told me the brother of my husband's killer worked with me. Wasn't that something I should have known about?

But sitting here holding the elderly woman's hand, he didn't look like an employee. He looked like a family member, intent on making a connection. In fact, he looked vulnerable, young and handsome. His dark hair fell just over his collar and his tanned skin was a warm, inviting contrast to his ice blue eyes. His lab coat hung on the back of the chair. Wait a minute, was I checking out the enemy? I coughed as I knocked on the door and stepped in. "Mr. Kelly, I hate to disturb you, are you doing a treatment? I can come back." Suddenly, as I looked at the name on the chart in my hand, it dawned on me. Mary Kelly, was Daemon Kelly's mother! No wonder I hadn't made the connection; there was no mention of Spencer anywhere on her chart. Also, he didn't resemble his bother … unless you really looked hard.

He turned and looked at me. "No, you can come in. Actually, I'm not working. My shift ended at three. I'm visiting my mom."

I blushed under his intent gaze and tried to distract myself by looking at her chart. "She had a stroke two days ago, the day of the sentencing," I said, then looked up, my eyes meeting his.

"By the way, I want to apologize for following you that day. I was way out of line," he said, then turned his attention back to his mother. The pain in his voice pulled at my heart. Like it or not, I felt for him.

I walked farther into the room and replied, "It's okay. That day was trying for both of us." Then, my gaze fell upon his mother, laying helplessly on the bed, asleep. "How is she?" If I kept the conversation focused on the patient, I could justify my concern.

"Hard to tell," he said, looking back to his mother. "She hasn't tried to communicate since the stroke. It was always touchy before with the Alzheimer's. I just hope that whatever reality she's in is better than this one. Knowing all this about Matty would kill her. Sometimes I feel like I've lost touch with reality, too." He said the last part more to himself than to me.

"I often feel like that, too, like I am losing touch or something," I said, looking at the frail woman lying helplessly on the bed.

He looked at me, holding my gaze with the cold blue of his eyes. "I don't know how you cope, how you do it. Maybe if I had been a better brother and not ran away from the situation I could have prevented all this," he said as sadness enveloped him.

I looked down, suddenly unable to meet his gaze. This conversation had taken a way different direction than I had intended. The feeling of loathing was replaced by a feeling of kinship. How could I let that happen? I decided to change the subject. "Why didn't I know that you worked here? Couldn't that be seen as a conflict?"

He pursed his lips, quiet for a moment before answering me. "No one knew. My name was different from his. I was the only next of kin listed, power of attorney, health care proxy … you name it. He didn't give a shit. I came home to take care of her a few months ago." He paused and looked at me before he went on. "But of course, now everyone knows after the news the other night catching me running from the courtroom. I'm surprised that you haven't heard the whispers. My days here are numbered."

I stepped closer to him, concerned. "Can they do that? I mean, you don't have any disciplinary problems, do you?"

He gazed at me thoughtfully. "That's a totally different response than I thought you would have," he said, then added with a crooked smile, "I thought you hated me."

"Well, hate is a strong word," I replied, giving him a weak smile. "I don't know you, as you had pointed out the other day. We could learn to work together peacefully … as long as you lose the deranged stalker deal."

At that, he looked at me and smiled a genuine smile, which made him look entirely too handsome. "I'd like that," he said sincerely.

I wasn't sure if I would, or could, yet. So I backed out of the room. "I have to finish my rounds. Goodnight, Mr. Kelly," I stammered.

Becca Boucher

"You can call me Daemon," he called after me as I hurried from the room.

As I walked down the hall, the conversation with Daemon left me seriously conflicted. I found myself wanting to know more about him ... his brother. Why was this happening? The worst part was that I couldn't get him out of my mind. When I went to bed that night, I found myself thinking about what it would be like to hold him. And for the first time in months, I didn't dream.

Chapter 7

Daemon

I heard her heels click against the linoleum floor as she hurried down the hallway, and her perfume lingered in the room. I wanted to call her back, to tell her I needed her, but I had already said too much. I was feeling vulnerable and alone. The last two days had been hell. Between the sentencing, the hospital and my mom, and the fact that I had started drinking again, it was the drinking that bothered me the most.

I had given it up in my first year at MA General. I hated who I was when I drank, too close to Matty and my dad. But I woke yesterday morning, leaning against my truck in the parking lot of Fosters' Mountain with two empty bottles of Jack next to me and a killer headache. I remembered starting up the trail, but how I got back ... well ... that was another thing altogether. I had no memory of that.

Now, as I sat in the dim light of my mother's room, I was bombarded with memories, like it or not. Long ago I had learned to push the memories away, thinking that they would kill me, like daggers to my soul. But now, I put my head on the edge of my mother's bed and let the memories flood my mind. They were all there ... a reel of movies playing at fast forward within my mind. The day my dad first hit mom, and the day he made me drag beer bottles to the redemption center in the snow. The day he walked out, the rifle he gave us for Christmas, and the first time he took us hunting. Mom ... the first night Matty came home drunk ... Melissa the day

I told her it was over … and, most vividly, the night of the murder. I closed my eyes and let the thoughts carry me away.

Kevin had just moved into my mom's house with me. He had fallen on hard times with his girlfriend and needed a place to stay. It was mid-afternoon and we were standing in the driveway drinking a beer, trying to decide whether or not to bring the U-Haul truck back or wait until the next day. Then, Matty pulled up, looking like hell. Unwashed, unshaved and smelling like old sweat and hard liquor, he was the last person we wanted to see.

"Well, look what the cat dragged in," Kevin said, and I hit him on the arm. "What? If that's Matty, then he looks like shit … worse than the last time we saw him. What do you think he wants?"

I pursed my lips and stared over Kevin's head at Matty. "Money, for sure, and to cause trouble if he heard that I was letting you stay here."

I watched Matty cross the lawn and something told me that this was going to be bad. "Hey guys, what are you two up to? I was thinking of picking up my guns and doing some hunting. Wanna come?"

I noticed that he swayed more than the wind and he shouldn't even be driving. I took a deep breath, knowing what was coming. I hated confrontation. "You haven't hunted in fifteen years, Matty. What brought this on? Why don't we just get some lunch and hang out?" Good … good … defuse the situation.

But Matty looked from Kevin to me with the manic eyes of a dope addict, unfocused and dangerous. "So, now you're the better hunter, too, D? I see how it is! I see! College boy comes home to save Mom and tries to save me, but you won't even let me move in, will ya, D?" Then he nodded to Kevin. "You take care of your buddies better than your brother?" He shot Kevin a warning look as he stepped closer to my side. "Well, if you won't give me my guns, I can always go in and take them." He stepped closer until we were nose to nose. "They're mine." Then he stepped back a bit. Kevin's fists clenched at his side and I shook my head slightly at him, stopping him. I had this. Then, Matty continued, "You see, I need some money, too, and I thought you could help me out with that ... seeing as you got the house, and all. Mom always left a little aside for me."

God, the difference between us had never been more evident. I had pushed my demons down and moved on, but Matty had given into his. I looked at the ground and slowly raised my head to meet his eyes. As soon as I said the words, I knew I was after a fight, letting my resentment do the talking. "Why do you have to be so much like dad? When life gets hard, you run and hide in a bottle. You never took care of Mom. I was the one running back and forth from Boston, taking care of her. Anything she gave you was out of fear ... fear and love. She always thought you could be better than dad, but all you did was disappoint her," I said, clenching my fists at my side, ready

He turned briefly before raising his fist and cocked it back as anger spewed from his mouth, "You son of a bitch! You always had to take it all! You always have to be better than me!"

I felt the punch connect as I lunged forward and tackled him to the ground. Kevin was behind me, pulling me off him, but Matty would have none of that. His strength out did me on a good day and, fired up with drugs, Kevin and I together were no match for him. He punched us both in a blur and we lurched across the lawn. I groped at anything I could find and my hand connected with a rock, but Matty kicked Kevin's legs out from under him and managed to knock Kevin on top of me before I could raise it. Kevin used all the strength he had and pushed us both back from Matty. I was slightly aware of Kevin's yelling as I dabbed at my swollen eye.

"What the hell, Matt? Take whatever the hell is yours and leave before I call the cops!" I said, standing up on shaky legs. "Take whatever the hell you want, but don't come back here and don't think you're getting a dime from me. Try getting a job!"

Matty walked right up to me until our faces were inches apart. I could smell the liquor and stale smoke on his breath. "You had to take it all, didn't you, Daemon? Well, you're no better than me! Yeah, you're some hero for coming home to take care of Mom. You're a big man with your college degree, dropping out of pre-med saying 'boo hoo, poor me.' Well, we all know that you just wanted to get away from your whore of a wife!" he said. Pushing past me, he ran into the house. I tried to go after him, but Kevin held me back.

"Let it go, man," Kevin said, pushing against my chest, forcing me to look into his eyes. "He's a piece of shit, Daemon! You have nothing to prove to him or anybody! He's talking crap and you know it."

The sound of things being thrown around the house rushed to us and a moment later, he stormed back out carrying the shotgun and rifle that dad gave us for Christmas fifteen years before. I didn't even know the last time it was fired. I had my own guns for hunting. Thank God they were locked in the garage. I had forgotten about this one. I watched as he got in his car. I barely heard Kevin as he shouted warnings at him not to come back and that we were calling the cops, but I knew that something else was making me feel uneasy.

The rest of the day I was consumed by the same uneasy feeling, knowing that something was going to happen. I questioned letting him walk away with the guns, knowing that it wasn't a good idea. When I called the police, they took it as a fight between brothers. But when they found out that he didn't have a permit or an FID card for the guns, they put out an APB on his car. My accusation of his drug use was secondhand, though, as I had no proof, so they told me to call right away if he came back.

That night as we drove back from returning the U-Haul truck, I studied the roads, looking for Matty's car. It was mid-November, pitch black and cold and Kevin's hands were white-knuckled on the steering wheel. "You mean to tell me there's nothing those cops can do? We told them a crazy guy, high on God knows what, was driving around with two guns and they say call back if he shows up again? Public servants at their finest right there, my man."

I shook my head and chuckled without humor. As much as I agreed with Kevin, I knew legally their hands were tied, as sick as it seemed. "I should have never let him leave with the guns, Kevin. We should've stopped him. I'm partly to blame for getting him going," I said, looking out the window.

"And have him kill us?" Kevin snorted as we pulled into the driveway. "There was no stopping him, D. You always take the blame. Give up the martyr routine all ready." I looked at my best friend and was ready to lay into him for getting on my case, too, but he was right. I had to give up taking the blame for everybody. Right then, Matty's car came screaming up to the curb. It was trashed, windshield shattered, and the hood was caved in. Parked half on the sidewalk, he left it running and jumped out. He flew into the yard yelling, and something red was all over his shirt. "You've got to hide me, man! Just until this blows over. Come on, I'm jacked man, woo! Flying high! What a rush, you know?" he yelled across the lawn, not caring who heard him.

Then the clouds moved, revealing a full moon, I saw the gun in his hand. I was slightly aware that Kevin had gone in the house, but I was more aware of the crazed look in Matty's eyes. "First of all, I don't have to do anything, least of all, hide you. Secondly, the way you came down the street the whole damned town knows you're here."

I looked at his shirt and the realization that it was blood hit me. I was hoping it was animal blood when Matty grabbed me by the shirt. "Look Bro, I am the one with the power right now, the one with the loaded gun. And I've got money! You hide me or you're dead," he yelled, then shoved the barrel of the shot gun cold against my temple.

I looked him square in his eyes. My medical training took over and I noticed the difference in the size of his pupils. "What did you do, Matty?" I thought quickly. "I'll help you, Matty. I promise. What are big brothers for? I just need to know what we're dealing with. Are you hurt?" I noticed the blue lights flashing in the reflective windows of my truck and tried to come up with more, wondering if he was buying it.

"You'll help me?" he asked, letting the barrel of the gun slip down just a bit. "You would do that for me?" Then, the police cars rushed the street and the police jumped out and ran into the yard, yelling for him to put the gun down. He looked at me hard with pain in his eyes. "You bastard!" Was the last thing he said to me before he pulled the trigger. I sucked in my breath expecting to die, but the chamber was empty. The gun clanged to the ground as the police pulled him off me.

The sound of the night nurse coming in to check my mom woke me, bringing me back to the present. What time was it?

She looked at me as I picked up my head. "You look like hell, Daemon. Go home and get some sleep. Are you working in the morning?"

I looked at my watch. It was a little after midnight. "No, I have second shift tomorrow," I replied. It was a good thing. I felt like I'd been hit by a train.

"She's sleeping," the nurse said, patting my shoulder. "I'll call you if anything changes."

I nodded my head at her and walked out the door. It was dark as I made my way across the parking lot to my truck. I was a little unnerved. I shouldn't have allowed myself to conjure up the memories. Just as I reached my truck the clouds shifted and the moon showed through, bright and clear. I think they call it a harvest moon at this time of year.

It was then that I saw him, standing at the back of my truck, waiting for me.

"Can I help you?" I asked.

The man looked up at me. He was so pale in comparison to the black clothes that he was wearing that the moon made him look translucent. He took a step forward before he spoke. "I hope so. You see, I noticed you were following Lilly the other day, and I don't like that. I'm watching her, too, you know. I would hate for anyone to take her away from me."

I shook my head in an effort to clear it and studied him before I spoke. "Who are you? Do you work here? I really don't like where this conversation is going, and if I see you around here again, I am going to call the police. She's had enough trouble for one life time."

The man took a step toward me and laughed, then he stepped into the moonlight so that his face was illuminated, most unnaturally. "Let's just say I watch over what is mine. And before I go, I know where he got the gun." Suddenly, the clouds shifted and the man walked back into the shadows, gone before I realized what had just happened.

Chapter 8

Lilly

I was awake this time. I was sure of it. Whatever I heard had made me sit bolt upright in bed. Whatever had made the noise was in the room with me. The second thing I noticed was that the cloud cover from earlier in the evening was gone and the moonlight streamed brightly into the room through my window, illuminating the chair in the corner and the figure sitting in it. Before the scream left my lips, he was sitting right next to me, holding his hand over my mouth. His voice was unmistakably Aaron's. "Shhh, baby. It's me. I didn't mean to scare you."

It couldn't be. Dreams were one thing, but seeing him when I was fully awake meant another … I was crazy. I tasted the salt of my tears as they made their way down my face and felt his hand move to my leg. I looked at him. "You can't be here. You're dead," I whispered, unable to believe what was happening.

"No, baby. I am here. I'm here from the other side. I've seen it, and I think you should come with me. That way, I can't lose you. They can't take you away from me," he said, looking into my eyes.

I shook my head, willing my sanity back. "From where? Who's taking me where?" I managed to get out through my shaking.

"With me. Back to the other side of the moon. There are more like me trapped in this void between Heaven and Earth. I was wrong, Lil. There *is* something out there, and you have to see it with me. You can help us get out; she told me so,"

Aaron said, running his fingers softly down my cheek, tracing the tracks of my tears. "She told me when I was still alive. She explained it all to me. Together, we have the power."

I pushed off the bed and ran toward down the hall, screaming behind me, "*NO!* You can't be here! You're not real!" I ran into the bathroom and slammed the door behind me, flipping on the light simultaneously. I jumped in the shower, nightgown and all, turning on the water as high as it would go. I stood in the shower, letting the water run over me until I was numb with cold and shaking.

After a while, I reached out and turned off the water. Stepping out, I shed my wet clothes and wrapped a towel around myself, sure that I now had a hold on my sanity. I sat on the edge of the tub weighing my options and decided that if I had been sleepwalking or dreaming, I was awake now. If I had been awake before … well … I didn't even want to think about it. Seeing ghosts was a whole new level of crazy. I pulled the towel around myself tighter and crept out of the bathroom and across the hall. I walked into my room and took it in, empty and quiet. The green numbers on the digital clock said 12:30 a.m.

I forced myself into the room and pulled on a pair of old sweat pants and a T-shirt, then grabbed my Bible. I crept downstairs—turning on the lights on as I went—and sat on the couch. Pulling my knees onto the couch under me, I opened the Bible to Corinthians and started to read. When the first light of dawn peeked in my windows, I finally fell asleep.

Chapter 9

I woke curled up in a small ball on the corner of the couch. My neck was stiff and I was unsure of the time. The phone started ringing and I forced myself up to get it.

"Did you forget to come to work today?" Kat's voice was icy with irritation on the other end of the line.

I shook my head. "No, I overslept. What time is it?"

She laughed, and the warmth came back into her voice.

"Nine-thirty in the morning, my friend. I guess you did oversleep. Have a fun night last night?" she asked, amused.

I smiled in spite of myself. "No, I wish! I just had trouble sleeping. I am on my way. Tell Nick I'll work late tonight to make up the time," I said, feeling every ache and pain from having slept on the couch.

There was a pause on the other end of the line before Kat spoke. "Are you sure you're okay? Do you need me to come over?"

I took a breath, forcing my voice to sound positive. "I'm fine! Just tired, is all. Now, let me get off the phone and get ready for work."

Kat gave a not-too-convincing laugh. "All right," she said. "I'll get Nick off your case. See you in an hour."

I hung up the phone, pushing back a sob; I was anything but fine. The thought of going upstairs to get ready for work had me shaking. And the icy tone Kat first greeted me with was sounding alarm bells in my head. All I wanted to do was to go back to sleep. When I was asleep, I could forget everything, that is, if I didn't dream. So I stalled, making a cup of coffee. Then, I looked at the paper without really reading it and made a fifteen minute chore of feeding the cat.

But if I wanted to get to work sometime today I had to go upstairs.

At the top of the stairs I paused to calm myself, and walked down the hall into my room. It was quiet, empty and sane. In the daylight last night seemed like it never happened. I must have been asleep. I picked out my clothes and walked into the bathroom. Making quite a production of the mundane.

As I dressed, I gave myself a pep talk. "Lilly, sleep deprivation is giving you very vivid dreams. You are not crazy! Aaron is not here!" I said aloud, trying to convince myself. As much as I missed Aaron and felt like I had unfinished business with him, I was starting to feel as if I wanted to move on. I would always love him, but seeing ghosts that want me to come with them was not my idea of moving on.

I tried to remember all of my college psychology classes and decided that it was my self conscious trying to punish me with that mind over matter crap. I looked myself over in the mirror. I looked pale, with medium-toned skin, shoulder length brown hair with a touch of blond and my green eyes. I suddenly found myself thinking weather Daemon was attracted to me or not and reached for my makeup. Looking back at the girl in the mirror, I told her that she had a right to be happy.

I had to admit that I was attracted to Daemon, which went against all reason. Besides being the brother of my husband's killer, he was what? At least five years younger than me? But what was five years in the scheme of things? Was I ready to live again? As I thought the question, I knew the answer. I thought I was and something deep inside me told me to give Daemon a chance. Maybe if I started living again, the dreams would stop.

Walking out of the bathroom I felt better, convinced that the events of the night before were nothing to worry about. I was always good at talking myself back off the ledge. This time, it seemed more important than ever.

By the time I got to work, it was close to twelve and the parking lot was full. I had a hard time finding a space to squeeze the Volvo into and ended up on the back side of the parking lot. I was thanking God that I hadn't brought the Camaro. The parking lot was so full that it was an accident waiting to happen.

Kat had told Nick something to convince him that I was working the later shift today, meaning, I had to stay to eleven tonight, making the location of my present parking space even more annoying. I was complaining about it at break with Kat before she left … and got no sympathy.

"Well, really Lil, if you had made it in on time this wouldn't be an issue. You're really cranky today," Kat said, pointing her car keys at me to accent her point. "I think you need a date. The recluse routine is getting old. Let me fix you up, I have this cousin, you know, the insurance guy? And I think it would be good for you to get out of the house."

I pushed the cover down on my coffee a little harder than I had intended, cracking the Styrofoam and cursing under my breath. "No Kat, what I really need is sleep— dreamless, peaceful sleep—and a best friend who was a little less of a nag."

She pretended to be upset. "Well, fine. Be like that," she replied, pretending to pout.

As she turned to go I said something I knew I was going to regret, "Plus, I have my eyes on someone."

Kat stopped in her tracks and turned on her heels with a sparkle in her eye. "Really? Oh, do tell."

I checked my watch to give myself time to take a deep breath. "Well, he works here. He's a tad bit younger than me and works in nursing."

Kat tapped her head in a exaggerated way. "Well, that narrows it down, since there are only three male nurses here.

Hey, you don't like a girl, do you?"

I threw my napkin at her. "No! Kat, you're really a jerk sometimes. It's a guy and he usually works second shift," I said, pretending to be real intent on fixing my coffee cup. "In fact … um … we kind of ran in to him before … at the court house."

I truly didn't know why I was saying this as my cheeks grew hot. The look on her face was no longer teasing; it was a look of recognition and distaste.

"If you mean the stalker brother of a killer, then I am seriously going to have you committed." She took in my silence for a moment, then continued, "Honestly, Lilly, if you're even considering that you have a screw loose. His brother is a murderer. He's the brother of a man who ruined your life, for crying out loud, and you find him attractive? Did Aaron mean nothing to you?"

I felt my face heat with rage as tears pool in the corners of my eyes. I set my coffee down and walked right up to her. "How dare you, Kat! Aaron meant the world to me. You know that! So much so that he haunts my dreams and now my waking hours! I spend day after day thinking that I'm going crazy. I see and hear him. This goes beyond normal grief. How dare you! And you don't know Daemon. I don't know him, but he said that he's nothing like his brother, and that could be true. I have a feeling that I can trust him. In fact, something is drawing me to him."

The look on her face was of utter betrayal, maybe even disgust. She spoke with measured words. "Well, I'm glad you have a *feeling*, but Aaron was my friend, too. I loved him, too, and this conversation sickens me. You be careful, and whatever feeling is pulling you that direction, I hope it's right. Because you can't expect me to come pick up the pieces and mourn for you, too." With that, she turned and stormed from the cafeteria.

I remembered the first fight that Aaron and I ever had. It

was over something stupid, like working over a holiday, but it turned into this festering wound that went on for weeks. Neither of us wanted to admit that we were wrong, so it went on until the holiday had come and gone and we had forgotten what we were fighting over. I was hardheaded, and he was a man! It was a conversation about the phases of the moon that broke our silence.

Aaron was convinced that the moon controlled everything. Not just waves and tides, but attitudes and emotions, physical cycles and energy. So we must have been in a phase of the moon that was negative, and once we were in a new moon, we were able to communicate better. I remembered how he took my hand and pointed up toward the sky, tracing the path of the stars, then kissed my fingertips. He was so absorbed in the sky that his anger faded, and it was contagious. We made love that night on a blanket in the yard while he whispered tales of ancient Wiccan rites.

He didn't believe in traditional religion like I did. In fact, he never gave much thought to the afterlife. He just thought your energy left your body and transferred to something else, back to the earth. I liked to think there was something more, a final destination for our souls. If he was right, then this was it. The here and now was all that mattered, and I found that hard to take.

I stood, walked across the room and found myself looking at the moon through my office window. It was almost a full moon. Aaron would have called it a blood moon or a Hunter's moon. He knew all the names of the phases of the moon and the corresponding dates. As I gazed out the window, I was beginning to feel bad about my fight with Kat. Maybe she was right, I had spent all morning convincing myself that I wasn't crazy. Now, I wasn't so sure.

I was thinking about calling her when a voice from the doorway behind me made me jump. "I'm sorry. I was just surprised to see you here so late. Can I come in?" I turned around to see Daemon standing there. He was still in scrubs and sneakers, and his dirty blond hair was slightly tasseled. His eyes were so blue and earnest that they caught me off guard. I found myself staring into them longer than was necessary, but it was as if I was looking into the windows of home.

"Are you okay?" he asked sincerely. As soon as he said the words, I realized that my eyes were wet with tears.

I wiped at my face, "Um … yeah. I was just looking out at the sky and got caught up in a memory," I said, clearing my throat. "May I help you?"

He took a few steps into the room before he spoke. "I was just surprised to see you here so late. Are you working over time?" he asked in a kind voice.

"I came in late so I'm staying late to finish some paper work. Are you leaving now?" I asked, but as I spoke, I realized that I hoped he was staying … and all thoughts of Kat vanished from my mind.

He looked kind of embarrassed when he answered me. "I saw you here and remembered something from last night that unsettled me. Would you mind if I walked you out to your car? I know it's really random, but I saw someone strange in the parking lot last night and … well … really, I would feel better." The look on my face was probably incredulous; I was trying to find the right words when he went on. "I mean, I understand if you don't trust me or feel strange, but then let me get one of the other guys from maintenance to walk you out."

"Okay," I replied, against my better judgment.

It was his turn to look surprised. "Okay, I can walk you out? Or okay for someone else to?" he asked hopefully.

I laughed. "Yes, you can walk me out. When are you leaving?"

I liked the way his eyes looked when he laughed. "Why? Are you excited to leave?" he asked.

I shot a quick glance out the window. "No, I just need to get my stuff together." I wondered if he caught the double meaning in my words.

"I'll meet you here in about thirty minutes. I have to give a report. Be good," he said, winking as he walked out the door. Yeah, now I really needed to question my sanity. A half hour seemed like a really long time.

As we walked to the parking lot a while later, I was careful to keep a respectable distance between us, but I kept stealing sideways glances at him. He had changed from the scrubs to jeans and an expensive looking Patriots Sweatshirt. With his untied sneakers and baseball hat pulled low over his eyes, he looked less like a nurse and more like a college kid. He was tall—taller than Aaron had been—I barely made it to his shoulder. He was muscular and ... he saw me looking at him.

I stifled a chuckle and the words came out of my mouth before I could stop them. "How old are you?"

It was his turn to laugh. "Direct and to the point, aren't you? I'm thirty. And yourself?"

I moved a little farther to my left. "Thirty five."

He stopped and looked at me. "Really? I thought you were much younger. Thirty yourself, at least. Maybe twenty-eight."

I wondered if he could see me blush, the moon was so bright. "Well, some days I feel ninety ... and I can tell that you're trying to butter me up."

We started walking again and I barley heard him when he spoke again. "I don't know how you do it. I feel for you."

I stopped at the back of the Volvo. "Do what?"

He looked up at me, searching my eyes for something. "Go on living with all that has happened. I mean, some days I want to kill myself for not stopping him, and here you have to live with this great loss, but you go on."

It was my turn to look down. I was uncomfortable with where the conversation was going. I didn't think I could tell him that I felt responsible and that I hid in my house for weekends at a time, or how I was seeing my dead husband in my dreams and now when I was awake. But at the same time, I was feeling this pull to Daemon. I wanted to keep him talking to me and, I hated to say it, but I didn't want to be alone again. His eyes were so earnest as the moon reflected on them. I quickly changed the conversation.

"Tell me, what was this strange occurrence that made you so intent on my safety tonight? Or was it an excuse to be alone with me?" I teased, trying to make my voice sound light.

He looked around him, scanning the parking lot. "When I left last night there was this guy by my truck. He was just odd looking, and he told me to stay away from you ... that he had to protect you. And he said some other things that were just off. It made me uneasy. Please, don't be scared. I don't see anyone here now, but we can call the police if you like. I promise that I'm not making this up."

He must have noticed the change in my expression and the concern in my eyes. All I could think of was my encounter last night. I managed to choke out, "What did he look like?"

Daemon regarded me for a second with a concerned expression. "I didn't mean to scare you ..." he stammered.

"Tell me what he looked like!" I demanded again, a little too forcefully.

"He was about 5'9", 190 pounds and all dressed in black. He was blonde, but the weird thing was that he was so pale ... almost translucent. At first, I thought that he was an albino for a minute ... and then he ..." I didn't hear the rest of his sentence before I fell onto my car and had to sit down on the pavement, as black spots appeared before my eyes.

Chapter 10

Daemon

"*Lilly?*" *I asked.* Kneeling down next to her, I pulled her hands from her eyes and held them in mine. "Lilly, what's wrong? Are you hurt?" I instinctively checked her pulse and searched her eyes for any sign of distress.

Her pulse raced beneath my fingers when she raised her eyes to mine. "You'll think I'm crazy ..." she said, her voice barley a whisper as the wind picked up around us.

I was suddenly cold, and left with a women who I was certain I had feelings for, although I had no idea why. She was a woman who was looking up at me with uncertain eyes filled with pain and fear. Was I ready to take this on? She pulled her hands free from mine and stumbled to her feet, backing slightly away from me.

"It was Aaron. You saw him! I saw him, too, last night. He appeared to me in my room ... our room ... and asked me to come with him. Oh, my God! You must think that I'am crazy." She turned from me and rested her head on the side window of her car. I touched her shoulder and she recoiled, shaking from cold or fear, I wasn't sure which. I tried to sound reassuring; whatever she was dealing with was real to her.

"Lilly, I don't think you're crazy. But, I *am* worried about you," I said, then turned it professional. "Your pulse was racing and you're cold. Do you feel like you are coming down with something?" She shook her head in a small quick movement. "Please, look at me." She turned, and this time when I took her hands she didn't move away from me.

"I'm not crazy ... really," she said, her voice merely a whisper.

I stepped closer to her and replied, "I know. The mind is a powerful thing, and if you are starting to get sick and fatigued, it can play tricks on you. Trust me. The person I saw wasn't Aaron."

She looked down at our hands, closed around each other. "But what about who I saw?" she asked, "and these dreams I've been having? Also, why would anyone care if you talked to me?" Then, she looked up at me as tears cascaded down her cheeks and said, "I don't want to be alone anymore." I don't know why I did it, but I pulled her to me, and my arms encircled her, pulling her close to me, and I rested my chin in her hair.

And she responded, leaning up against me with a sigh. I took in the feel of her in my arms, smelling the perfume on her skin. "If you can trust me, you won't have to be alone." I didn't know why I said it or why I felt this way, but I knew it was true. I was just as damaged as she was. All reasoning and decorum told me that I should walk away, but I couldn't. I was cemented to this time and place, and something outside me told me to watch over her. I didn't think that I had anything to give. I thought I had left it all upstairs in my mom's hospital room, or in the dark night with Matt's sins, but she pulled out the best of me from deep inside.

Before I knew it my lips were on hers, and her hands were tangled in my hair as our bodies pressed against each other. She pulled me closer, parting my lips with her tongue as she held onto me for dear life. I don't know how long we stood there like that, but the moment was broken by a gust of wind and the feeling of icy cold, vice like fingers were suddenly on the back of my neck. A feeling of dread pulsed through me and I jumped back from her, fully expecting to find someone behind me, ready to confront the intruder.

"Daemon, what's wrong?" Lilly asked.

I spun around and the parking lot was empty behind me, except for leaves blowing randomly in circles around my feet. "I thought I heard something." I took in her face, uncertain and sad. Was it because of me? "I'm sorry. I shouldn't have ... um ... taken advantage of the moment like that."

She smiled, sad but sincere. "No, it's okay. I haven't been held in so long. I don't know what came over me, but it's okay. Please, don't feel bad. This night has been so strange. It feels as if you need to be here with me." We stood in the parking lot, taking each other in silently.

"I should go home," she said, then turned to put the key in her car door.

"No, let me follow you home. You had me scared a couple of minutes ago and I would feel better. Once you get there, I'll drive right by, I promise," I said, feeling an intense need to protect her. She nodded her head as she got into her car.

I drove my truck in utter silence, totally fixated on the tail lights of Lilly's car in front of me, like a beacon, leading me toward a new life. I started this evening thinking that I would find a bar on the way home and get wasted. Now, I was thinking that I really wanted to take her out for coffee. I wasn't sure if I was sent to save her, or if it was the other way around.

Suddenly, I felt the ice cold gust of wind again. I reached back behind me to close the sliding window and found it stuck. As I went to put my right hand back on the wheel it jerked suddenly to the left, propelling my truck into the oncoming lane of traffic. I jerked hard to the right, going off the shoulder of the road into soft dirt. It was then that I noticed the dials on my instrument panel spinning wildly. Voltage, gas, temp, they were all going back and forth, blinking in protest. I struggled to control the truck, but my power steering was gone. All of a sudden the truck jerked to a halt, throwing me against the steering wheel. "What the hell?" I asked as my eyes shot up to see Lilly's car nowhere in front of me. The road was deserted.

I reached across the seat for my phone, and found myself in the icy-cold grip of a pale hand. The passenger side door of the truck opened, and the rest of the body came into focus, pale and glowing. "Who are you calling, Daemon? Could it be someone I know?"

My stomach lurched, making me feel sick. "Who are you?" I demanded as fury filled my body.

"The lady already told you who I am," he replied, laughing. "I thought I told you to stay away from her. I tried to play nice, but it seems that you were not paying attention." He pulled open his shirt, reveling gray skin, punctuated by a jagged hole in his stomach.

I recoiled backward into the driver's door. "Stay the hell away from me! Oh man ..." The sound of my voice seemed far away. I reached behind me to open the driver's door, and fell from my truck into the road. I scrambled backwards, getting to my feet. "What do you want from me?" I screamed into the now empty truck. I could no longer see because of the thick clouds that were drifting across the sky to cover the moon as I ran to the other side of the truck. "What do you want from me? Show yourself, you bastard!" I yelled into the empty truck, looking like a crazed lunatic. There was nothing but dark night around me. I climbed back in the truck and rested my head against the steering wheel. "It can't be." I reached up and turned the key, and the truck roared to life, running smoothly. Disbelief clouded my vision as I opened the door and retched violently into the road. I didn't know why, but I had to get to Lilly ... and fast!

"This can't be real!" I repeated to myself over and over as I sped down the empty road to Lilly's house. "Like you told her, you're tired, sleep deprived. Oh man, I need a drink!" Where could she have gone? I wasn't stopped that long, she only had ten minutes on me. Turning down her street, I half expected to see her just ahead of me. The street was empty of life. Pulling in her driveway I saw the Volvo parked and her house was dark.

I pulled to a stop. When I got out of the truck, something felt wrong. I just couldn't put my finger on it. "Lilly?" I shouted at the dark house, walking to the front of her car and called a little louder, "Lilly, are you okay?" I noticed that the door to the garage was open and the lights to the Camaro were on, illuminating the backyard. I peeked my head in the door and called again. "Lilly! This is not funny, where the hell are you?" The door to the Camaro was open and as I walked in I saw her purse on the front seat with the keys dangling in the ignition. Then I saw her coat lying in the backyard, and further down in the bushes I saw a figure lying still on the ground. "Oh, my God, Lilly!" I yelled, running across the lawn to her, expecting the worse. I felt as if I was starting to lose my grip on sanity; I would have given anything to be drunk at that moment.

Chapter 11

Lilly

Looking in the rear view mirror, I no longer saw the lights from Daemon's truck. I felt foolish for missing them; they meant comfort and caring, but he owed me nothing. I didn't know how I felt about the kiss. If I was truly honest with myself, I liked it. It felt like home, like I wanted to be with him, but admitting that seemed like a betrayal to Aaron for so many reasons. Actually, being with anyone felt like a betrayal. Kat would tell me that I needed to get my head straight before I could see anyone. Seeing my dead husband was probably a turn off to most men. If she knew how badly I was messed up, she would flip!

As I turned in my driveway, the cold night air seeped into the car. I reached up to turn on the heater, when I noticed that the garage door was open and the Camaro was turned around. How could anyone have done that? The hair stood up on the back of my neck. I parked in the driveway, got out of the car, and headed to the house with every intention of calling the police.

"Lilly …" Aaron's voice called to me from the shadows of the garage.

"Aaron?" I asked, starting toward the garage, gripped with fear. Every inch of me told me to run into the house, but my body kept walking toward the garage. That's when the line blurred between dream and reality, when I lost touch with what was around me, when I saw something I never wanted to see. I was trapped in a dream and I could see, hear, feel and smell everything, but I was stuck in my own mind.

Suddenly, I was standing in the street in front of the package store. A dark shadow in the snow filled the night. I looked up and Matthew Spencer got out of his car, leaving it running in the parking space closest to the door. He pulled the shotgun from the backseat and loaded it. I tried to stop him, but he walked into the store, anyway. I was invisible to him. I rushed to the store window as he pointed the gun at the cashier, emptied the cash drawer, and struck the man with the butt of the gun. I pressed my palms to the cold window and watched as he trashed the store, then packed his pockets with anything he could reach. I cringed and jumped back when he looked right at me, but he saw nothing.

I heard the roar of the Camaro as it pulled into the store parking lot, and my stomach fell when I turned to see Aaron get out. I ran up to him and tugged on his arm, trying to get his attention, but I was nothing but a wisp of smoke in a dream. Then, he walked up to Matthew and confronted him. I screamed for him to stop, the soundless scream that fills your mouth in dreams and leaves you gasping for breath. I watched as anger filled Matthew's eyes, the rage of addiction. Suddenly, he raised the gun as Aaron reached for his cell phone. As if in slow motion, Matthew fired the gun and blood spewed from Aaron as he fell to the cold ground.

I stumbled and slipped as I grabbed for him, but could do nothing, watching helplessly as the car raced away. Onlookers pulled up, jumped from their cars and tried to revive Aaron. A guttural scream rose from my lips that no one could hear. Rage filled my body as I suddenly felt myself being propelled down the street away from him.

A group of kids were saying goodnight on the sidewalk. Cody, a teenage boy, started to cross the street, but turned back to respond to his friends. I screamed for him to get out of the way, but the car slammed into him. I slid to the cold ground and rocked back and forth, begging to wake up as I watched Cody's body hit the pavement with a thud. Then, it was dark and silent.

Suddenly, I was sitting in the Camaro. I felt the coolness of the leather seat under my hands as light flashed before my eyes, as if signaling the end of a movie.

"Is this the kind of family you want to be associated with? Did you see what he did to me?" Aaron's voice punctuated the blackness, making me even more confused and scared.

"No! Leave me alone!" I yelled as I ran from the garage and into the pitch black yard. Clouds covered the moon that I so lovingly looked at earlier. "Leave me alone! I can't take this! I don't want this! Why are you doing this to me?" I ran until I fell down the slope of the yard and rolled into the bushes. Finding myself unable to breathe, I closed my eyes and begged and prayed. "Please, God, Please! Make it stop!" I begged as sobs rocked my body.

Daemon

She was lying on the ground, curled into a ball under the bushes, crying so hard that she didn't hear me approach her. "Lilly? Lilly, are you hurt? What's wrong?" I asked, placing my arms around her. She looked at me with unseeing eyes.

It was hard for me to make out what she was saying through her sobs ... sobs that quickly turned to soundless shudders. "Don't leave me alone. Please!" she managed to get out.

I picked her up and carried her toward the back of the house as so many things were running through my mind. Did I want to get involved with this? Was she loosing it? Was I? I mean, I saw something back there on the road behind the airport, didn't I? But when I thought about leaving her ... of turning away and doing my own thing ... it felt wrong. I just couldn't leave her. In that moment, I knew I was staying. "Lilly, I'm going to take you in your house, is that okay?" She nodded into my chest. "Okay, you have to tell me where your keys are."

"In the Camaro ... in the garage ... but I don't want to go in there again." Her voice sounded tired as she said it. I wished that I could see her face.

"I'll get them, but I have to leave you here by the door. Is that okay?" I put her down as I said the words. She held onto my hand for a long second before she let go and nodded her head in agreement. I walked into the garage and took the keys out of the ignition. Glancing back at Lilly huddled in the porch light, I knew whatever had happened to her was connected to what I saw back on Marshall Street; I was sure of it. I closed and locked the garage and made my way back to the house. "Which key is it?"

She took the keys from my hand and picked one out. "I think I can do it," she said, looking at me hard. "I thought you changed your mind and went home. Something happened. I'm so afraid." She looked at me and wisps of her hair were coming out of her pony tail, her shirt was untucked, and her eye makeup was running down her cheeks along with her tears, but she still looked beautiful ... and vulnerable.

"Of what?" I asked, my voice barely a whisper.

Hers was even softer. "Of Aaron."

The door opened into a comfortable kitchen. She crossed the room, then sat at the table and put her head in her hands. I closed the door behind us and turned on a lamp by the window before I sat down across from her. "Can I stay? I mean, I know it's imposing of me to ask, but I don't want to leave you alone. I saw something on the way here. Something strange happened and I don't know if it relates to what happened to you but, I'm worried about you ... and me."

She raised her head from her hands. "I saw him." She said it simply, as a matter of fact. "Tonight ... again ... but tonight was different. The other times, I always thought I was dreaming because when I woke, I was always in my bed and it was always at night. But when I came home just now, it was as if I was sleep walking. He was here and ..." She cracked her knuckles and looked at me with pleading eyes. "Please don't think I'm crazy, but it was like he took me back to the night he died. I saw every detail, everything I never wanted to see ... I saw him die," she said as tears streamed down her face.

I reached across the table and took her hands; they were cold. She put her head down, leaning on our entwined fingers. The room was comfortable and homey, my eyes rested on the antique clock on the wall above her, checking the time. I took a deep breath and said, "My first instinct is to say maybe you were remembering details you heard at the trial ... getting mixed up ... but I saw him, too. I was following you home and we were just out of the city, on Marshall Street, when my truck went off the road and conked out. Then, someone got into my car ... someone ... not alive. It was the same man I saw at work the other night. I was totally freaked out. Then, I came here and couldn't find you."

She looked up at me and silence filled the room and her eyes hardened. "Don't even try and tell me that." She took her hands from mine, "Don't even try to gain my trust by making fun of me and saying that you saw him, too. Don't you dare!" She stood up and walked to the door and flung it open. "You can leave now; you have no right."

I stood up and went to her, trying to think of a way to convince her. "No, Lilly, I'm telling you the truth. Please ... please believe me. It scared the hell out of me. I threw up right there on the road."

Something in my eyes must have convinced her; maybe it was the pleading tone of my voice. She softly closed the door. "Was the moon out?" she asked.

I looked at her confused. "Yeah, I think today was the full moon ... if it's the twenty second. The moon was bright when we were in your office, before the cloud cover moved in." Now, our encounter in her office seemed like years ago.

She leaned against the door jamb, looking tired. "The moon is always out when he comes." She looked at me with a faraway look in her eyes. "Do you believe in God?"

It occurred to me that if I lied and told her yes, she would see right through me. It was so much more complicated than that. "No. I used to, back before my world fell apart. Do you believe in ghosts?"

She blinked and pursed her lips. "I never used to, but tonight was different. I feel like everything I ever believed was turned upside down. Yes, I think there are ghosts. Do you?"

The floor was suddenly very interesting to me. The inability to deceive her was so strong that I couldn't fight it. I looked up and met her eyes. "No, but something so strong is pulling me to you. Since the day of the sentencing, I can't stop thinking about you. I hear your name whispered in the wind, feel your presence in my room at night and, whatever it is I saw on the side of the road tonight, it was as scary as hell. After I saw it, all I could think of was getting to you. It might not be a ghost, but something otherworldly is going on here, and I think you know it."

She slid to the floor and placed her head between her knees. I had struck a chord with her. After a few long moments, the one word she said to me when she raised her head was spoken with conviction, no trace of doubt. "Stay."

I slid down next to her and took her hand. "Do you have any liquor?"

Chapter 12

Lilly

When I woke up the sun glinted through the window from the west, signaling that it was late afternoon. I sat sideways on the couch with my head resting in the hollow of Daemon's chest. He was in deep sleep, snoring heavily. There were two empty wine bottles on the floor with a few drops left in one glass on the coffee table. In the past, waking up in a situation like this would have scared the hell out of me. Now, I felt safer than I had in months. He was right. Whatever was pulling him to me was also pulling me in his direction.

I used the time in my half-awake state to study his features: his square chin and solid frame, the strength of his chest under me, the way his hair was sticking to his forehead as his eyelids fluttered in his sleep. He was tall, but not lanky; he was well proportioned. He smelled wonderful right now, a mixture of wine and some cologne that smelled like woods, musk and sweet herbs.

I snuggled onto his chest and thought about what we talked about last night when he got back from the store with the wine. Well, it was really the wee hours of this morning. He told me that he was agnostic, unlike Aaron, who didn't really believe in one God but felt that nature guided us and science could explain anything. Daemon felt that we were alone; there was nothing to believe in. We talked very little at first about what we had both seen in the way of Aaron. Instead, we focused on the pull we felt. He told me that when he had pulled up the night before and saw that my car was gone, it was like he had no other choice but to go after me, as if the choice had been made for him. He couldn't have turned around if he had wanted to. And as much as I wanted to say something else, the word 'stay' flowed from my mouth with no reservations. We discussed his mom, how he feared that she was in pain and couldn't tell him. He told me of her marriage, her fear, and how Matty started to run wild in high school. I told him of growing up as an only child, of finding Aaron, and that my first real friend was Kat. His eyes filled with rage when he told me about the night his dad left and how Matty had taken his side, running after his father and flipping off his mom.

When the second bottle of wine had started to take its effect and make us groggy, we talked of the ghosts, the ones we saw, the ones we battled … unseen. The question of whether Aaron's ghost was real or not remained unasked. I hoped it was the wine that was making me see shadows move in tangible forms around the doors and windows. When he took me in his arms I knew the pull was not imagined. I felt I was stuck to him with magnetic energy. Before we both had passed out, I delighted in the feel of his hands in my hair, whispering that I was okay, that I wasn't crazy, and that we would figure it out together.

I felt him start to stir under me the same time the phone rang. I ignored the first five rings and jumped when Daemon spoke, "Are you going to get that? It really doesn't help a hangover."

I snuggled deeper into this chest before I responded. "No, I'm too comfortable."

He chuckled as the phone went quiet. "Good afternoon, then," he said, pulling me closer to him. "I suppose we have to get up."

"Not if you don't want to. I could lie here all day," I replied. Then, I smiled up at him to drive my point home. Why was I feeling this way? Where was the remorse and betrayal I should be feeling? But I wanted Daemon here.

He looked at me with an intent expression. "Wow, then I didn't dream your sudden change of heart. I see I'm still welcomed." He changed his position to lean in for a kiss, the first since yesterday in the parking lot. But as he did the phone started ringing again. "Oh, my God, you really have to see who is calling you. I don't think they're going to give up any time soon." He flopped back down on the couch pillow with an exaggerated frown, closing his eyes again.

I pushed off him, making my way to the phone, and realized that moving was making my head pound severely. It appeared that Daemon wasn't the only one with a hangover. Hopefully this positive mood wasn't still due to the wine. My smile faded as I read the caller ID. Kat. "Shit," I said, frowning.

Daemon sat up and looked over at me. "What? Someone you don't want to talk to?"

"That's an understatement," I told him as I picked up the phone. "Hi, Kat."

She heaved a heavy sigh on the other end of the line. "Thank God you picked up! I feel so totally bad about yesterday. I guess you have every right to ignore me, but I thought for sure that you were going to call last night. What time did you get home?"

I debated about what I should tell her and looked over at Daemon on the couch, wearing a quizzical expression on his face. "After twelve. Look, I know things sounded bad to you, but I am okay. I have a lot more to worry about than whether or not you think it's safe to hang around with him."

Daemon raised his eyebrows at me and pointed to himself. I waved my hand at him.

"Well, Lilly, you just took me by surprise is all," Kat replied, indignant. "I mean, are you serious? You think that killer boy's brother is attractive to you?"

I looked over at Daemon, as he patted the couch seat next to him, and I had never been more confused … or excited.

"Hello! Lilly, earth to Lilly." Kat's voice was a mixture of venom and honey.

"I'm here," I said, not taking my eyes off Daemon. "I just have to think about some stuff … and I sort of have company." What was I going to tell her?

"Who?" she asked flatly.

I coughed, stalling, then answered, "Daemon. He followed me home last night … to make sure that I was safe. Kat, some strange things are going on and he's seen them, too. We got to talking last night."

There was total silence on the other end. When Kat finally spoke, she was more than pissed. "Really? And you couldn't talk to *me*? Well, that explains why you haven't answered the phone all day. Lilly, I won't allow this. I didn't give you Aaron to let you walk all over his memory."

Heat shot up through my veins, causing a sickening feeling to return to my stomach. "What do you mean 'give me Aaron'?" My voice barley registered in my ears.

I was doubtful she heard me as she continued her rant. "Whatever you're thinking about … whatever strange stuff that's going on … I hope it includes finding a mental health counselor!" Suddenly, the line went dead.

I closed my eyes and pressed my hand to my face. All of a sudden, I couldn't breathe. What was I doing?

Before I knew it Daemon had his arms around me, whispering in my ear, "What was that about? It sounded pretty intense. I hope I'm not the one causing trouble in that conversation."

When I looked up at him, he looked as tired as I suddenly felt. I searched my mind for the right words to reassure him, when suddenly a chill went through me and I felt a release of tension, almost a calming feeling wash over me. The word 'truth' echoed through my mind. "Yes. You were." He stiffened in my arms. "But, I don't care." I surprised myself with this statement, because as I said the words, I believed it. "My friend, Kat, thinks that trying to be friends with you is wrong ... a betrayal to Aaron."

Daemon pulled back to look at me. "And what do you think?"

I glanced around the room, the setting sun was casting a late fall glow through the windows. I felt a presence I couldn't put a name to, as if someone was watching us. I shook my head to bring my thoughts back to the question. "I think she's wrong. I think it's out of my control. But, most of all, I think that we have something to offer each other." I didn't know what I meant by "out of my control."

Confusion registered in his eyes, then he suddenly smiled. "Well, that, I think we have something in common that we can't name. Maybe it's stress causing us to see things to confront our fears, but I don't think we should tell your friend or anyone, for that matter, that we're seeing ghosts." He made a joke of it, but part of me was worried that he didn't believe me, that he might have humored me last night.

Cold replaced my calm feeling as Kat's words also echoed through my mind. "My friend Kat has also been saying some things that are setting off bells ... weird things ... like that she gave Aaron to me. I'm so confused, Daemon." A little tremor shook me.

He took my hand, concern in his eyes. "What does that mean?"

I just shook my head, wishing that I knew.

"Are you hungry, Lilly? I can cook, you know," Daemon said, pulling me toward the kitchen.

"Yeah, let's eat," I said with a smile, brushing Kat's words from my mind.

As I sat at the table I was surprised at how at home Daemon was in my kitchen. It was as if he had worked in it before. He found everything that he needed for a simple, delicious dinner without even asking me.

We ate in silence, each lost in our own thoughts. I was feeling light headed, attributing it to the lack of food and the abundance of wine I had in the wee morning hours, but when my vision got blurry and light seemed to glow around Daemon, I became worried. Suddenly, a strong feeling of déjà vu washed over me, as if I had experienced a quiet evening with him before. As the feeling of calmness and peace spread through me, I could see a vision—as if looking though a kaleidoscope, fragmented and colorful—of a man and woman sitting by a fire. I realized that I had closed my eyes and opened them to find Daemon staring at me.

He reached across the table to take my hand and asked, "Are you okay? You seemed far away for a moment?"

I shook away the fog that had clouded my mind. "Yeah, I think that I'm just feeling the effects of the wine. I need more food in me. Want me to make dessert?" I got up from the table and felt his eyes follow me as I started cleaning the dishes. I got the feeling I was starting to believe in the supernatural. I looked over and the shadows in the corners danced.

Chapter 13

Daemon

At eight that night, I left. I told her I had to go home and let Kevin know I was still alive and check on my mom, but really the fact that I was falling for her scared the hell out of me. I wasn't good with relationships. Hell, I was still trying to get out of the one with Melissa ... and I hadn't even told Lilly about her yet. But what surprised me the most was how hard it was to leave. I felt like it was wrong, as if someone wanted me to stay with her to protect her.

Even backing my truck out of her driveway was like pushing against a magnetic field. I didn't get it. And the fact that she seemed so preoccupied when I left was not sitting well with me, either. No, I didn't think she was crazy. We both saw something last night and there was no logical explanation for it, and I kept getting this weird prickly feeling that told me we were both in for a shock ... and that we were in it together, like it or not. In the span of three days, I was questioning everything that I believed ... or didn't believe. I was also certain that Lilly wouldn't like the idea of me watching over her. She was too independent for that. Suddenly, my cell phone rang as I turned down my street.

"Hey, I was wondering if you were still alive! Where have you been, man?" Kevin said with a teasing tone in his voice, probably thinking that I was on another one of my bar raids.

"I was with Lilly. I'm actually headed down our street now. What's up?" I asked, trying to sound nonchalant.

"Lilly? Who the hell is Lilly?" Kevin took in my silence and made the connection. "The widow. Man, I'm not shocked at all."

Suddenly, anger rose up within me. "Don't say that again! It's not like that with her! She needs me and I need her; I don't know why." I hung up on him as I pulled in our driveway. What was I doing? What was it about his comment that angered me?

Kevin met me on the porch in the fading twilight. "Say what again?" Kevin looked clueless, but started apologizing anyway, "I'm sorry, man. I didn't know *how* it was. You look like hell, by the way."

I figured I did. "I fell asleep on her couch last night ... well ... early this morning ... after a lot of wine. I think I need some time alone to think," I said, knowing that I sounded as confused as I felt.

Kevin leaned against the railing, watching me with a strange look in his eyes. "It's not weird? I mean, she's not freaked out by the brother of her husband's killer thing?"

Sitting down on the top step, I pondered what he was saying. Was it weird? To me it was feeling entirely too comfortable ... and right ... but I detected no note of accusation in Kevin's voice. "No, I had some car trouble, she got locked out of her house, and then we ended up helping each other." I rested my head on my knees. It was *close* to the truth, anyway. "Like I said, I need to figure some things out for myself before I can talk about it."

Kevin avoided my eyes, looking out over the trees across the street. "Are you drinking again?"

His simple question could have summed it all up and it should have been the question to make me mad, but I answered it anyway, looking down at to my feet. "A little."

Kevin slapped me on the back. "All right, brother! I'm headed off to bed. I have the early shift. With it being Sunday and all, who the heck else would want it? If you need me, wake me up."

Kevin was like that, not prying. Anyone else would have started giving me the third degree, but that simple question let me know what he thought. The friendship was so easy and safe. It was the one relationship that I had been able to keep for years, but I wasn't ready to tell him about seeing ghosts and supernatural feelings. Could it have been because I was drinking again? No, I certainly wasn't drunk when I first saw the ghost back on Marshall Street yesterday. And that ghost—Aaron or not—had seemed real to me.

As I looked out at the night over the tree tops, I realized that I was starting to believe what I had seen. It should have scared the hell out of me, but instead, it filled me with a longing that I couldn't put a finger on. A thrill of adrenaline came over me every time I remembered Lilly's head resting on my chest in the early morning light.

Yawning, I walked straight back to my bedroom, eager for some sleep as thoughts of Lilly filled my mind. I lay down on the bed, thinking of her, when my cell phone rang abruptly, bringing me from my reverie. "Hello?" It was hard to keep the cell phone from slipping out of my hand in my half-asleep state. "Mom? When did she start talking?" I asked as I jumped from the bed. "I'm leaving now! What do you mean 'she wants to bring Matty flowers'?"

The nurse on the other end said, "She keeps asking for lilies. Then, she asks for Matty. Is that your brother? She keeps saying it over and over, and she's getting really agitated." I pinched the bridge of my nose. "Give her the PRN Ativan she has ordered. I will be there in thirty minutes." I clicked the phone shut and fumbled for my car keys. My mom was talking! Not only was she talking, but she was forming coherent sentences!

Part of me was wondered if the end was near. She hadn't talked in a year … well … before the stroke. And to start talking out of the blue, asking for flowers for Matty? I couldn't fathom it.

Running through the kitchen, I stopped and opened the fridge and fumbled toward the back. "Damn it! Where is the beer?" As the last forty-eight hours ran through my mind … well … I needed a drink. Turning toward the cabinets, I remembered the Captain Morgan in the cupboard over the sink. I pulled it down and took a long gulp straight from the bottle. Suddenly, warmth made its way through my body, calming me instantly. I took another long swallow and, even though I knew better, took the bottle out to my truck with me. I tucked it under the seat and started the truck.

Half way down the block I took another gulp and put the bottle back under the seat. I saw the pink glow of dawn and glanced at the clock on the dash, five thirty in the morning, almost time for the day shift. Was Lilly working today? I was starting to feel the familiar warmth of liquor seep into my thoughts when my cell phone rang again.

"Hi, I hope you don't mind that I called," Lilly said. "I wanted to make sure you were up for work. You mentioned last night you were working the day shift today." She sounded worried. I coughed to clear my voice, suddenly wishing I had breath mints.

"Actually, I am on my way there as we speak. Amy, the night nurse, called to say that my mom was talking up a storm. Are you okay?"

Silence.

"Lilly, you there?"

"Yeah," she said, sounding like she felt better. "I was just unsure if I should call is all. I didn't want to sound desperate."

I had to chuckle. "Lilly, you lack self-confidence. Of course it's okay for you to call! You can call me any time day or night. Where are you?" I could almost guess from the way the phone reception sounded.

She was breaking up when she answered, "By Crown Hill Disk Golf. I should be turning into the parking lot anytime now."

Hunting the Moon   71

"Wait in the lot for me?" I asked, smiling.

It took her less than a second to answer. "You don't have to ask me twice."

Ten minutes later, I pulled into the lot and she was resting against the side of her Volvo. The sight of her brought back the feeling of longing, and I was kind of pissed that I had to park four spots away from her. I forced myself to walk at a reasonable pace and started toward her.

When I got to her, it looked as if she stopped herself from giving me a hug; her arms were slightly raised. "Is your mom okay?" From the look in her eyes, she hadn't got much sleep, either. They were rimmed with dark circles and she was pale.

"Yeah," I said as I stepped close to her. "She started talking out of the blue ... real random ... she really hasn't been coherent in about six months ... and she was asking for flowers for Matty." At the mention of Matty's name she cringed. I cursed myself for being so careless. I stepped closer to her. "I'm sorry. I shouldn't have."

She backed away from me". What the hell, Daemon! Did you fall asleep in a bucket of Jack? Is liquor your idea of breakfast? It's six o'clock in the morning!"

Shit. I stopped in my tracks. "You can smell it?"

In spite of herself she smiled. "Yeah. Unless you want to get fired, you might want to take care of that." She fumbled in her bag and took out a package of gum. As she tossed it to me I noticed a cut on her arm. "How did you do that?"

She pulled the sleeve of her sweater down. "I'm the one asking questions here. Eat the gum before we go in. Is this a habit of yours?"

I chewed a second before I answered her. "No. It used to be. Truthfully, I don't know how to answer that."

She regarded me for a long moment, then took my hand. "What are we doing here?"

Suddenly, it was my turn to be thoughtful. "I don't know that any more than you do."

She laughed. "What the hell do you know?"

I looked at my watch. "I know that if we don't get in the door and punch in, we're going to be late. I know that they're waiting for me in my mother's room ... and I know that the blonde over on the other side of the lot is giving me a dirty look. That must be Kat." As we walked toward the door, Lilly looked over her shoulder.

"Yeah, that's her. She's probably ready to call the psych ward for me, but I could care less." She squeezed my hand. "I'm worried about why you're drinking at six in the morning, though."

I was trying my hardest not to get resentful of her questions. At that moment, a wind picked up and gushed across the lot. Suddenly, a cold burst slammed into my back and I shivered. Lilly looked at me. "What was that shiver for?"

"Just the wind," I said, reaching down to squeeze her hand. She looked at me quizzically.

"What wind?" she asked with wide eyes.

As she looked at me, I realized that the air was still, despite the cold-as-ice feeling on my neck. All of a sudden, I didn't know what to say.

She took a deep breath. "Are you okay to work? You're not too drunk, are you?"

I pulled my hand from hers a little too roughly, and my voice was a little too hard. "Is this twenty questions? Of course I'm okay to work. Taking two gulps of rum before I left the house doesn't make me a damned drunk."

I saw the tears in her eyes a little too late, then she turned and marched toward the door. The shape of her back, her hair falling over the collar of her coat, and the quickness of her steps away from me made my heart ache and filled me with dread. "Lilly, please wait. I'm sorry. Please, Lilly, don't go in mad."

She stopped and spoke over her shoulder. "It's okay. Go check on your mother. I'll find you later."

I really hoped that she would. As I watched her walk away, another cold wind struck me in the parking lot. "Please, Lilly," I whispered to the empty air.

No one was in my mom's room when I got there. The light was low and the curtain was still pulled over the window. I walked over to her and placed my hand softly against her forehead. She stirred in her sleep. "It's okay mom, it's Daemon. I heard that you had a bad night," I said, taking her pulse as I watched her breathe. She seemed peaceful in her sleep. "Why are you worried about Matty?" I held her hand. "He can take care of himself, Ma." I was thinking that I should go find the floor nurse to see if she had taken her meds and maybe check her chart when I heard an unfamiliar voice behind me.

"How is she?" The voice was in no way friendly despite the question, and I jumped as I turned to see who it was. It was Kat. Her expression told me sthat he was not going to take any shit from me. She went on before I could answer. "Not that I really care. I mean, I care about the residents, but you, I could give a shit about." She walked farther into the room. "You see, I can't figure out why you're hanging around Lilly. Maybe you're in league with your brother and this is part of a sick game, or maybe you just get off on Lilly's pain. I don't know, but she looks like hell this morning and I don't think she really knows what she's doing."

I stood and started to speak, but she was hell-bent on not letting me.

"Don't bother! Don't bother trying to win me over. If you hurt her, I'll kill you myself. Aaron's death will not be in vain," she said. When she turned away, I grabbed for her arm. She looked down at my hand on her wrist with disgust.

I spoke trying to measure my words and pull in my temper. "Truthfully, I don't know why I'm drawn to her. I never started out to hurt her and I'll do my best not to. For the record, I'm nothing like my brother. You don't know a thing about me."

She pulled free and looked at me with hard eyes. "Really? You smell like a drunk and made Lilly cry. I saw her in the hall. And I know that you came back to town too late to save her." She pointed at my mom.

I looked over, pissed to see that my mother was awake with tears rolling down her cheeks. What had she understood? I looked at Kat, seething, losing my temper as the seconds ticked on. "Get the hell out of this room!" She looked at me with hard eyes.

"Gladly!" Kat yelled, storming out of the room and down the hall.

I turned my attention back to my mother. She was struggling to speak, and she was having trouble breathing. I reached for her call light. "Mom, it's okay. Shhh … just rest," I said. She gripped my hand and I leaned closer to hear her. She squeezed my hand firmly, looking directly into my eyes. "What did Matty do?"

I had to sit. It wasn't possible that she understood. She couldn't know about Matty, could she?

Suddenly, the dayshift nurse rushed into the room. "Daemon, is she okay? I gave her the PRN at the turn of the shift. What is her oxygen set at?"

I couldn't even answer her. My mind was spinning.

"Daemon! Are you okay?"

I looked at her, unable to answer.

Another nurse came into the room and spoke to me. "Daemon, they want you down in HR. The Director of Nursing is down there, too."

I looked at both of them and sprinted from the room. "Let me know if my mother's condition changes," I yelled over my shoulder, halfway down the hallway. For a minute, I didn't know what I should do. Part of me wanted to run from the building, but the logical part of me knew that I needed to stay and calm down. I stopped, leaned against the wall and pressed the heels of my hands to my eyes, concentrating on steadying my breathing and my shaking hands. Why did they want to see me in HR? This could not be good.

When I walked into the HR office, I was met by the Director of Nursing, my supervisor, and the HR director. As soon as I walked in the door, my boss closed it behind me and I was asked to sit. Carol, the HR director, cleared her throat and started the conversation. "Daemon, we know that you have been well liked here. We gave you a chance, since you had no long-term care experience. But, it has come to my attention that you have been drinking on the job. And that you are somehow connected to the murderer of one of our dietician's husband." She perched herself on the edge of her desk and looked me straight in the eyes. I couldn't hold her gaze. My head was spinning and I was starting to feel sick.

I felt a hand on my shoulder. "If you had come to us sooner, Daemon, we could have resolved this. A situation like this can be awkward for everyone involved. Just how are you connected to the murder case?" I turned my head to see it was the DON, Deb, who had her hand on my shoulder. It was slightly comforting and ominous at the same time.

"My brother was convicted of killing Lilly Lawson's husband," I said, looking at the carpet. "Our names are different. We've been estranged. I didn't see the need to make a big deal of it."

Carol's voice was as cold as ice when she responded. "I'm sure that you can see how wrong you are. If you had been up front with us, we could have taken the proper steps to reduce the impact to our staff."

I felt the anger rising in my stomach, making its way up to my shoulders. I tried to slow my breathing and calm myself. "No, I don't see how it impacts the staff. Is it going to impact the care that my mother receives? Are you going to spread the news around so that she is known as the mother of a murderer?" I glared at her, boring my eyes into her very soul. "I'm sure you can see why I kept the information to myself."

She rose from her desk and walked across the room toward me. "I don't like your tone, Mr. Kelly. And when it evolves into an improper relationship with another staff member, it most certainly does impact the staff."

I rose myself, my face turning red, ready for a fight. "What I do on my personal time is none of this facilities business! Who are you to decide what is inappropriate or not?"

"Daemon, it's okay," Deb said. "We're just trying to figure out if there are any conflicts of interest. Carol, I think we're getting off track here." I turned toward Deb, my eyes pleading with her to be on my side.

Carol however, was not backing down. "Mr. Kelly, you haven't answered the question of whether or not you have been drinking on the job. And, from the way your breath smells, I can make my own assumptions."

"I have not been drinking in this facility," I replied, looking directly into her eyes. "I've done nothing improper on the grounds of this facility, but I had a drink before I left the house this morning. Do I have a friendship with Lilly Lawson? Yes. But nothing improper has happened, and I have never come to work drunk." I punctuated my response by slamming my palm on her desk, shaking her coffee so that it spilled on a stack of paperwork in the corner. "Never! And I would love to know who has given you all this information, because I can harbor a guess as to who it was."

Carol looked at me with hard eyes. "Well, your behavior tells a different story. I'm sorry, but I'm going to have to terminate your employment here effective immediately."

I sank back into the chair as only one thought came to mind … my mom. I turned my attention back to Deb, focusing only on her, fighting to stay calm. "My mom. Can she stay? Will I be able to visit her?"

It seemed that everyone was trying to talk at once. "We will make exceptions for your mother. Usually in these situations we would ask you to move her, but in this case, it would cause her more harm. You will be allowed to visit as long as you make no attempt to contact Ms. Lawson on facility property."

I looked at Carol, void of all emotion, trying to hold on to myself, to be rational.

"I'll have to ask you to leave for today, though," Carol added.

Without another word, I stood and walked from the building without looking back. I was numb. As I walked across the parking lot, I saw Kat standing in a window, with a grin a mile long plastered across her face.

Chapter 14

Lilly

When I finally found Kat, she was standing at the window in our office. I had no idea why she was looking out for me, and after the last few conversations we had, I was in no hurry for a confrontation. "Kat, Nick said you were looking for me. What's up?"

She cleared her throat and turned to look at me. "I thought I should be the one to tell you. I was the one who talked Carol into it."

She wasn't making a lot sense to me. I narrowed my eyes and glared at her.

"I guess I'll come right out and say it," Kat continued. "Daemon Kelly was fired about twenty minutes ago. This is going to make it so much easier for you. You won't have to deal with him talking to you and trying to get all buddy, buddy with you. In fact …"

I cut her off mid sentence. "What?" By that point I had crossed the room and was right in her face. "What do you mean 'he was fired'? What did he do? Or, better yet, what did you do? If you ask me, this has your meddling ways all over it!"

She took a step back from me, shocked. "Meddling ways? If you call keeping you safe from that train wreck meddling, than whatever! I was going to tell you that you can get a restraining order now and he wouldn't even be able to visit his mom. Which, really, if he is a drunk is it any big loss?"

Her words stopped me in my tracks. "A drunk?" I asked,

unable to believe what I was hearing. "Where did you come up with that idea, Kat? Is that what happened? You ran off to HR with some half-spun rumor?"

She actually looked hurt, her perfectly made-up eyes dangerously close to tears. "I saw you come in from the lot after you walked in with him. You were crying, Lilly. Whatever he said to you upset you. Then the guys up on five cleaning the floors were talking about how he smelled like a bar room. I put two and two together. If you ask me, he got away with working here for far too long."

So that was it. My suspicions were true. "You had no right! He wasn't drunk! Yes, he had a drink this morning, but he was certainly not drunk. And you have no idea why I was crying! Did you ever think ..."

"You are terrible at lying, Lilly," Kat said, cutting me off. "You always were." I looked at my "best friend," at her perfect makeup, her day spa haircut and tailored suit. She was always well put together and up on the latest fashion, the total opposite of me and my Target sweater and pants. In fact, she was always telling me that I needed to be more "refined." Like the toast she gave at my wedding. Everyone thought she was joking when she made fun of our choice to camp in the Maine woods for our honeymoon, rather than go lay on a beach in Bermuda. The truth was that she was really mad that we chose the camping trip. She even offered to pay for our honeymoon if we went somewhere she thought was "appropriate." Kat was the beauty queen, married to the lawyer, and I was the ordinary friend. Well, this time she had crossed the line. She cost a man his job because she didn't approve of my choices.

"Do you really know me Kat? Because you don't know Daemon. After all these years, you still think you have to mother me," I said, finally seeing her for who she was.

Kat looked at me hard. "You don't know him, Lilly," Kat said, her face cold as she stared into my eyes.

"Well, give me the chance to get to know him," I said, suddenly trying to be the voice of reason.

Kat put her hand on my arm. "As your friend, I'm telling you that it's wrong."

I pulled free of her grasp. "Why? Because of what his brother did? Or because I should be mourning Aaron for years to come? We shouldn't judge people by the sins of their fathers … or their brothers."

She reached for me again. "Lilly, you're betraying Aaron. The man we loved."

Tears started to cascade down my cheeks. "We? You don't have any idea of the nightmares I live through: the lonely nights in my bed, the guilt, the pain. Don't you dare tell me that I'm betraying Aaron because I struggle with that daily, whether I'm dating Daemon or another guy. And for you to say that you had that much love for him? You have some nerve Kat."

She looked at me as her eyes glazed over with tears. "We had something, Lilly. I wanted …"

I couldn't believe my ears. What she was implying? I didn't want to hear one more thing that she was saying. "Go to hell, Kat!" I ran from the room, shaking with anger and fear.

I spent the rest of the day avoiding Kat and losing myself in care plans. I tried Daemon's cell once from work and it went straight to voice mail. Struggling with wanting to find him and not wanting to look desperate, I felt like I was sleepwalking through my day. At four o'clock I found myself waiting to leave, but I didn't want to go home. That's when I made the decision to go see his mother.

When I got to her room, the late autumn sun was setting through her window. She was sleeping, covered by an old quilt that looked homemade. The room was warm, and filled with books and pictures. Daemon had obviously made the effort to surround her with things from home. I searched for his face in the pictures, and was taken aback when Matthew's face looked back at me from two pictures placed far back on the dresser. I wanted to take them and throw them through the window, but when I picked one up, I was fascinated by the boy who looked back at me, before his face was hardened by drugs and time. He was holding his mother's hand and staring right at the camera, almost challenging whoever was taking the picture. He must resemble his dad, because I saw none of Daemon or his mom in his face.

I jumped a little when I heard a small voice behind me. "I was wondering when you would come see me. It's been such a long time." I turned and Mary Kelly smiled at me, a smile that was so much like Daemon's that it brought tears to my eyes. "Can you stay a while? We have so much to catch up on."

I smiled back at her as I crossed the room to her bed. "I think I can," I said, sitting down on a chair beside her bed. "I have nowhere else to be."

She smiled and reached for my hand. "Good. Should we put on some tea?" she asked.

Her face was so sincere that a chuckle escaped my lips. "I think I've had enough tea today. How about we just talk?" I pulled the chair up closer to the bed.

She had a smile that lit up the room, and you almost forgot that she was locked in the prison of Alzheimer's disease. "Well, you look tired. Did you make dinner for the boys last night? The light was on so late."

"No, I just had trouble falling asleep," I said, playing along. Something inside me opened up, knowing that it was safe to talk to this lady. She would never judge me, or remember what I said. "The dreams have been so bad. Sometimes I think I'm going crazy. In fact, I think he is really there, more a ghost than a dream."

She patted my hand. "A little bit of tea always helps the baby sleep." I smiled and looked into her eyes. "In fact, Lilly, you always had trouble sleeping when the moon was out."

My face must have fallen to the floor and was two shades of green because I stood up in such a hurry that the chair fell backward to the ground. "How do you know my name? Why did you mention the moon?" Backing to the door I saw her face fall. "Where are you going? We have to pick the flowers for Matty."

Oh, man! This was getting weirder than I would have ever thought. Panic rose within my chest. Running down the hall, I heard her faint cries to come back. I needed to get out of the facility; I needed to find Daemon.

This time when his phone went to voice mail, I left him a message. I told him that I saw his mom, that I was worried about him, and that I needed to find him. I had no idea where he lived, just that his roommates' name was Kevin, so driving to his house was out. I circled the back roads around town until the moon was high in the sky. When I saw no sign of his car, I searched the two liquor stores in town. I just went where my soul led me. In fact, I felt pulled by some guide, as if I was not in control of where my car was driving. By midnight, I gave up and headed for home. I felt so alone when I pulled in the driveway that I sat in the car with the radio on for another hour, afraid of the silence that waited for me in the house.

The moon was so bright that the path to the door was glowing and I had no trouble getting the key in the lock. I wasn't hungry, just tired, longing to get into bed and work out all the emotions in my mind.

As I made the way up to my bedroom, I could hear music playing. I followed the sound down the hall to my room and discovered that the clock radio was playing softly, the sounds of a classical waltz. I thought it was funny, because it wasn't my usual station. I must have changed the station when I went to shut the clock off in the morning. I put on the low bedside lamp and drew the shade down. A strange feeling, not quiet *de ja vu*, pulled at my consciousness.

I was aware that I was missing something, but what it was, I didn't know. It was as if the key to where Daemon could be was looked up inside me. I didn't feel that he was in trouble. It felt more like that he didn't want to be found at the moment, as if he was on a momentary respite from the pain. But which pain?

Sleep. That's what I needed to escape my pain. I lay in my bed, clothes and all, and begged sleep to take me from the emotions of the day, leaving the classical music on to lull me into the darkness.

Whether I was awake or dreaming, I had no clue. It was so real that I could see and feel everything, but it was like watching a movie with the sound off. I saw a lady rocking a child by a fireplace. She fingered a necklace of the Madonna and Child around her neck, humming a low lullaby too quiet for me to make out. The room was comfortable and homey. An older boy sat playing on the rug with matchbox cars lined up around him. A TV was low in the background. I stood in the corner like a silent interloper.

The woman turned to look at me, but looked right through me. Mary Kelly's face smiled down at the boy on the rug. Suddenly, the quiet was broken by the slamming of the front door. For a second, the boy on the rug looked excited by whoever was coming home and ran to meet him, but the man ignored him and walked to the chair where the woman was rocking.

Their words were too low for me to make out, but the woman was hurt by whatever was said. The man stepped over to the boy on the rug, then went into the kitchen and got a beer out of the icebox. He came back into the room and sat on the couch. The boy ran over to him and tried to climb onto his lap, but was swatted away by a hard hand. The man wanted quiet, not to be disturbed. His day had been too hard and long, but the boy persisted in trying to tell him whatever was on his mind. He pushed the boy away and told him to shut up, so he could hear the TV.

Becca Boucher

Suddenly, anger filled the room with yelling and commotion. I held my hands to my ears and willed them to stop. They were scaring the boy and the baby was starting to cry. For a moment, it was as if I was disconnected from my body. I wanted to wake. Part of me knew that I was sleeping. Then suddenly I was sitting in my bed as a stream of bright moonlight filtered into the bedroom through the window.

It took me a moment to make sure that I was in my room, but was I awake? I heard a low voice next to me, whispering The Lord's Prayer. The shade that I had pulled closed earlier was up, and in the shaft of light on the floor sat Aaron, praying.

"Aaron? Why are you praying? You never believed in it before?" I asked. I rose from the bed and walked over to him, where he was crouching on the floor in the moonlight.

"Lilly?" he asked, looking straight into my eyes. "Do you believe that I'm here?" He took my hand in his cold translucent one.

"Why, Aaron? Why are you here?" I asked. The moonlight made his skin appear to be blue. "I'm scared, Aaron. I need to know what's going on. Can you please tell me?"

His other hand reached out to touch me, and his finger lightly wiped away a tear from my cheek. "Yes. I can tell you a little. I need your help. I wasn't supposed to die like I did. Morgana told me that I had the power. That together we would find the answer."

He seemed real and imagined at the same time. I reached for his face, but held back. "Aaron, who's Morgana?"

He rose and reached out for my hand. "She's my teacher, my goddess. We were in love." My hands shook and as I stood face to face with Aaron. He looked to the ground and shook his head, speaking faster and more frantic. "I need to know why? Why the bastard killed me! You can help me, Lilly. Let the brother get close to you and find out why, but you'll always be mine. I will take you with me before I let him love you." A shock of light pierced my fingers where they touched Aaron's. "We were meant to go to Heaven together, that much I know. For a while I thought Kat was the key, but her bloodline forbade it. We were meant to be together."

I inched away from him, cold with fear. "Aaron, you're scaring me. Your telling me my worst nightmares. I don't understand."

He smiled and said, "Good. You *should* be scared. Fear is a great motivator, Lilly. There's so much more than we learn in church. The spirits are real and all around you; I'm not the only one. Did you know that angels don't always have wings? And some of them work for Satan. The fallen ones." Aaron paused as if hearing a command. "I've said too much."

A cold wind blasted through the window, knocking the lamp off the table. I was done. Dream or not, I needed to wake up. I pulled from Aaron's grasp and ran from the room. Tears ran down my cheeks as sobs rocked my body. Locking myself in the bathroom, I pulled the blade down from the top of the medicine chest and held it to my forearm, just under the old cut Daemon had seen. I put pressure on it until I felt the pain and saw the blood seep out, dragging the blade down just enough to see that I was alive. Feeling pain convinced me I was awake, but this time it took longer to feel the pain. This time, I pushed the blade deeper until my hand shook. In that moment I was detached, all I cared about was making the confusion in my head stop. It was almost a relief to see the blood. I dropped the blade in the sink and grabbed the towel off the rack and pressed it to my arm to stop the flow of blood. I sank to my knees, pressing my head to the floor and prayed. If I was going crazy, this was the worst way. I would rather slip into nothingness … anything but this.

All of a sudden, I thought of how Daemon's mom knew my name and I knew that it was connected to the dream. She was the woman rocking the baby. She was trying to tell me something. I rolled to my back and fell asleep on the bathroom floor. I didn't wake up until the sun filtered through my window and the ring of my cell phone vibrated on my leg.

I was stiff. By the time my brain registered that it was my cell phone making the noise, the call was gone. I heard the house phone ring from my room and groaned. It would have to wait. Looking down, I realized that the towel I had wrapped around my arm hours before was stiff with dried blood. Slowly, I pulled it off and I found the cut had stopped bleeding, but it was deep ... deeper than I had ever cut myself before. Man this was not good. It actually looked like it could use a trip to the ER, but I wasn't going there.

I took off all my clothes and ran the shower until steam filled the bathroom. Then I stayed in the steady stream until the water ran cold. I was avoiding whoever was on the phone, and whatever the day was offering me. There was only one person that I wanted to talk to, needed to talk to. I wrapped a towel around myself and walked across the hall to my room, taking inventory of the situation.

Sitting on the side of my bed I started to mentally check off all the things that I had tried to avoid. The signs were all there: the dreams, the visions, and the strange feelings and sensations. Aaron's ghost was real. I had seen him, Daemon had seen him, and he was here for a reason, but he was scaring the hell out of me. The second thing was the visions. I was seeing the past. Someone was trying to send me a message. Or were they trying to help me? And the third and last thing was the feeling that I was being lead or guided. When I was driving and looking for Daemon, was someone on the same side as Aaron guiding me? And what *was* Aaron's side? Was he here to save me or to take me from this world?

I looked down at the cut on my arm and saw the blood trickle from it again. I was so tired that I wrapped up my arm and climbed into bed. Whoever had been on the phone would have to wait. Daemon. When Aaron was still alive, I remembered reading about spirit guides and guardian angels with him one day, and I was suddenly sure that I had one, but who?

Chapter 15

Daemon

"*Where the hell is she?* Something has to be wrong," I said out loud to myself, frantic as I paced around the kitchen with my cell phone in my hand. I had just tried calling Lilly for the seventh time this morning.

"Why don't you just go over there if you're so worked up about it?" Kevin asked. "You should have picked up when she called you yesterday." I stopped in front of the window looking out over the leaves covering the backyard, dead and crisp as Kevin talked. "She's probably just pissed that you didn't pick up when she called. You get drunk, she gets pissed. Match made in heaven."

I turned and glared at Kevin. "I wasn't drunk."

He shook his head. "D, even if you weren't drunk, going into work, smelling like Captain and coke at six in the morning is not good. It almost seems like you wanted to be fired."

I was quiet as I looked at him. Once again, he stated the simple truth as only he could. I should have felt resentment, but I only felt empty. "I would've been fired, anyway. After her friend, Kat, stuck her nose in, they would have found a reason no matter what." I turned back toward the window. I never denied the drinking. I could have fought the firing, otherwise.

Kevin stood up and joined me at the window. "How well do you know her? You were honest and raw in front of her and you're in pain over her," Kevin asked, crossing the room to look into my eyes. "Do you love her?"

I stared out over the dying grass and leaves. Frost sparkled on the ground at the edge of the woods. The nights were getting colder. How could I explain to Kevin how I was feeling? I was being pulled toward her and pushed back at the same time, bound to protect her, but visited by the ghost of her dead husband who wanted me nowhere near her. I sounded more like a crazy man than a drunk. "I do ... and I have a feeling that something's wrong."

Kevin handed me a cup of coffee and stood next to me, silently looking out the window. "And?"

I turned my head and met his eyes. "Is it that obvious, man?"

Kevin chuckled. "You look like hell, you were pacing all last night, and you didn't even finish a beer I found warm in the bathroom this morning. And to be honest, when *you* leave beer lying around ... well ... something earth shattering must be going on."

I took a deep breath and rested my head on the cabinet above the sink. "Do you believe in ghosts, Kev?"

He was silent for a long minute before he spoke. "Like the guys in long white sheets, or the spirits that knock your stuff off tables in the night?" Kevin asked, considering the idea. "I never really thought about it."

I lifted my head and looked right at him. "How about God?"

Kevin stared at me. "Are you having some ethical issues with the widow? There will always be people that question your motives. Do I think you seeing her is wrong? I really don't know. I know who you are as a person and you would usually run the other way from this type of scrutiny, but really, I think it has nothing to do with God."

I looked into his eyes. How the hell was I going to tell him? "That's not what I meant. I feel like ... that I'm connected to her for a reason, and—I know this is going to sound absolutely freaking out there—but I think I've seen her husband's ghost. She had this episode where he came to her the same night I saw him and he took her back to the murder scene. It was all too real to be imagined. I feel like I can't leave her alone."

It was Kevin's turn to stare into the yard. He ran his hand through his spiky hair, lost in thought. Now that the gate was open, I had to continue to purge myself. "I love her Kevin, and there's no logical reason for it. I spent one evening with her and we talked into the night and I feel like I know her better than anyone else in this world ... except maybe you." He smiled a little at the comment. "I never believed in anything before: God, ghosts or anything other than taking care of myself. But now, I have this feeling that someone is trying to bring me to her ... and her husband is pissed about it. I know it sounds messed up, but man ..." I stopped talking suddenly, not knowing how to go on.

Kevin looked at me. "I don't know what to say, brother. I never would have figured you as a sucker for a girl-ghost love triangle." He smiled as he went on, but the joke was lost on me. "I don't think you're crazy. I don't know what to say about the ghosts, but I don't think you're crazy, man. I think that maybe fate put you two together. You can help her, and she can help you, but starting drinking again is a bad thing ... especially if you're going to start hallucinating."

I slammed my mug down hard in the counter and shook my head. I tried to keep my voice even, but I was getting pissed. "It has nothing to do with drinking. Just forget it!" I stomped toward the door. "I need some air. I knew you wouldn't get it."

"D, I am sorry," Kevin said, reaching for my arm. "But you toss this ghost thing on me and expect me to have an answer for you? You both have been through hell this last year and, frankly, I think she's good for you."

I looked down at the floor than back at Kevin. "Thanks." I was suddenly at a loss of what else to say. I really didn't know what I expected from him. It might have been easier if he had just called me crazy.

The quiet was interrupted by the ringing of the phone in my pocket. Looking at the screen, I recognized the main number of the facility. I tried to sound pleasant when I picked up the call, just in case it was about my mom. "Hello?" I didn't recognize the voice on the other end at first.

"So, where the hell is she?" The voice was distinctly female and really pissed sounding.

"Who is this?"

She laughed. "You know damn well who it is! Where is Lilly? She called in to work today and won't answer her phone and, if you ask me, it has something to do with you!"

Damn. It was Kat ... just who I needed to make my morning complete. But the fact that she was looking for Lilly quelled some of my anger.

"She won't answer my calls, either," I said. "What the hell makes you think I have something to do with it? I haven't talked to her since six yesterday morning ..."

"Yeah and she was crying after that," Kat replied, cutting me off in midsentence. You better stay away from her! I should have tried to have you fired two weeks ago after the sentencing ..."

It was my turn to cut her off. "So it was you! I had my suspicions. What does it matter to you who Lilly talks to? You made me lose my God damned job, Kat!" My grip was so tight on the phone that my knuckles were white. Kevin took one look at me and backed out of the room.

"Really? Your job Daemon? What about when it comes to her life?" Kat said, her voice rich with sarcasm.

"What do you mean her life?" I asked, starting to shake.

"I mean, when you make her forget Aaron. When she falls for you and you either leave her or kill her ... like your brother killed Aaron in cold blood!"

I picked up my mug from the counter and threw it across the room, shattering it on the wall and sending coffee all over the floor. Kevin came in and tried to put his hand on my arm, but I threw it off as I started my tirade. "You bitch! You know nothing about me or my brother! I would *never* hurt Lilly! Shouldn't you be more concerned about where she is than yelling at me? You'd better stay away from me and her!" I threw the phone across the room and it shattered when it hit the floor when a million more things that I could have said rushed through my mind.

"Is that what everyone thinks of me? That I'm the same as Matty?" I yelled at the top of my voice. "He tried to kill me that night, too! You were there, Kevin! He had the gun pointed at my head, pulled the trigger and it jammed! I am not like *HIM!*" I started to sob. All of the anger I'd been harboring since that night turn into rage. Even now, I was trying to push down the violent shaking that needed to destroy everything in the kitchen, and a stronger need for a drink. Kevin stood in the doorway watching as I sank to the floor and put my head on my knees.

All I wanted was Lilly. The need to have her with me was so great that I couldn't put a name to it. It was more than worry of what might have happened to her; it was a strong physical need. She would understand. She was the only one that would … or could.

I was aware of Kevin picking up my mess and trying to put my phone back together. I sat on the floor for what felt like hours with my head on my knees, wondering if this was what going crazy felt like. Finally, I looked up to see Kevin watching me. "I don't think we can save your phone, man."

I pushed myself up off the floor. "Probably not. I'm pretty good at destroying things. I need to find Lilly."

He looked at me with concern. "Then I'm going. Go take a shower. I'll get my jeep."

Thirty minutes later, we pulled into Lilly's driveway. Her Volvo was there, and I checked the garage to make sure that the Camaro was there, too. The house was dark. Even though the day was overcast and it was late afternoon, there were no lights on in the house. I led the way up to the porch and knocked on the door. After a few seconds, I knocked again. "Lilly? It's Daemon. Come on and open the door. Kevin is with me. I just want to make sure that you're okay." I rang the bell impatiently and, finally, I heard her make her way down the stairs.

She opened the door, took one look at me and threw herself into my arms. "Daemon! Thank God you're here." I held her tightly, burying my face in her hair.

"Kat called me."

She backed up and looked at me. "Kat called you? Why?"

I held on tightly to her hand. "She thought I had something to do with you calling in to work today. Do you know that I was fired?"

She looked over my shoulder at Kevin. "Is this your amazing roommate?"

"Yeah," Kevin said, laughing. "And today I'm his amazing chauffeur. Do you want me to go, D? I can come back and get you."

"No, stay. Come in … both of you," Lilly replied before I could. "I heard that you were fired today. Kat made a point of telling me right before she accused me of betraying Aaron again. Between that and the visions last night, I've had a wonderful time." She looked like hell. It was obvious that she had taken a shower, but her hair was still hanging in wet curls on her shoulders. Also, she was pale and had shadows under her eyes. Not to mention a big bandage on her arm. She had yet to let go of my hand and I wished Kevin would refuse her invitation to stay, but from the way we both looked and the breakdown Kevin witnessed this afternoon from me, I was sure there was no way in hell that he was leaving.

She led us into the living room and I held her back. "What's up with your arm?" S

he tugged the arm of her sweatshirt down. "Nothing. I fell on the stairs yesterday and scratched it on the railing."

I pulled the sleeve back up and lightly touched the bandage. "That's one hell of a scratch. Can I take a look at it?"

"No, really it's fine," Lilly said a bit too quickly, pulling her arm away. "I'm just so tired and with the dreams and all, I tripped on the stairs." She sounded like she was trying to convince herself even more than me.

We were interrupted by Kevin calling from the living room. "Really, I don't find this awkward at all … sitting here alone … all alone."

Lilly laughed and asked, "Is he always like that?"

Chapter 16

Lilly

Daemon and I sat on the couch hand in hand and Kevin sat cross legged on the floor. It seemed strange to be sitting there with the two of them while it grew dark outside. I had let Daemon take a look at my arm and he bandaged it a lot better than I had been able to. He said it could have used stitches and to watch it for infection.

As he tenderly held my arm I could tell that he didn't buy the story that I tripped on the stairs. We seemed to have an unspoken agreement that I wouldn't ask about his drinking, and he wouldn't ask about my arm. Just having him here was comforting, but the questions from the two of them hung in the shadows of the room, just waiting to be asked.

I studied Kevin when he wasn't looking. He was cute, but in a different way from Daemon. He was shorter, and his hair was that messy, spiky style that some of the younger guys liked. I could tell that he liked to joke around, but if push came to shove, he would have Daemon's back with no questions asked. While Kat would try to sway me to her way of thinking, Kevin would just back Daemon up, to be there for him. I was jealous of that. His brown eyes darted around the room and he tried to keep the mood light as we took care of my arm. Now, he was every bit as intense as Daemon as I tried to convey to them how unsettling my dreams were.

"I think maybe these dreams are a way of telling you that you are guilty about starting a friendship with D here," Kevin said as he traced a pattern on my carpet with his fingers. "I mean, I'm no shrink and I don't even play one on

TV, but it seems to me like a logical explanation." Apart from the humor that he was trying to inject into the conversation, I could see that he was really trying to help.

"I think it's more than that," I said, patting Daemon's hand, then I rose and crossed the room to close the blinds. "I was having the dreams for a while before the sentencing, before I even met Daemon. I'm sure that Aaron's trying to tell me something," I said, saying the last part more to myself than to them.

"And what about me, Kev?" Daemon asked. "I saw him when I was awake ... twice ... in the parking lot and on Marshall Street that night."

Kevin pushed himself up off the floor. "I don't know, bro. You just might be crazy." He laughed, but we didn't. "No seriously," Kevin began again. "I think you both are being too hard on yourself for wanting to start a relationship or friendship or whatever. You're just worried about what people in town are going to say. I say 'screw it'! Lilly, I just met you, but I know that you're good for D ... and I think you need him. You both need someone who has been through the same pain. No one knows Daemon like I do, and he's very different from his brother in many respects." He picked up his keys as he continued to talk. "D, you were talking about ghosts earlier and the jury is out on that one, brother. Don't get mad at me, but Lilly, he needs to stop drinking again. Watch him. Other than that, I have to get to work, friends. Night shift. You okay here, bro?"

Daemon looked up from his hands. He had been looking intently at his fists as Kevin spoke. "Yeah. I'll find a way home," Daemon said, rising to his feet.

"Don't worry, Kevin," I said, rising to my feet, too. "I can bring him home, or he can stay here." I looked at Daemon with hopeful eyes, having no desire to spend another night alone.

"All right, I'll see you guys tomorrow," Kevin said with his hand on the door handle. "Have a good one." Then, he turned his attention to me. "It was a pleasure to meet you, Lilly." With that, Kevin walked out the door, gently pulling it closed behind him.

I looked at Daemon and he met my eyes at the same time. "Are you mad at him?" I asked, searching his eyes for the answer.

He was quiet a second. "No. It's hard to be mad at Kevin. He's the most loyal guy I've meet, and he doesn't tell you only what you want to hear; he tells it like it is. Annoying? Yes, but it's refreshing. He's had my back for a long time … when I'm sober or not."

It was the first time that Daemon had mentioned his drinking to me. I sat back down next to him and he put his arm around me. "How much does he know? About us?" I asked.

He was quiet again. "He heard me go off on Kat today."

"You went off on her?" I asked in disbelief.

He kind of laughed. "Yeah, she said something to the effect that I was using you," he said, taking a deep breath. "My temper got the best of me."

"She means well," I said, leaning back against his shoulder, "but she never let me explain about us. I'm a big girl, but she likes to meddle." Meddle was too weak of a word to describe my so-called best friend. So many things seemed different to me now. I sighed and leaned against Daemon, then pulled my legs under me on the couch. He leaned back and pulled me onto his lap. It was comforting and natural in his arms. I finally relaxed.

"Kevin said ghost. Do you think that Aaron is a ghost?" I asked, then continued, "because that's what I think. Last night, I saw him, heard him, and almost touched him. It was much more real than a dream. The air gets so cold and I can feel my skin tickle. It frightens me."

It took so long for him to answer that I thought he had fallen to sleep. Or maybe he resented that I was talking about

Aaron. I was so relaxed, taking in his warmth and his scent, that he startled me when he spoke.

"I hate to admit it, but the times I've seen him, he was so pale and cold. Hell, I never saw him in life, but after talking to you, I just knew it was him. When he showed up those two times, I felt icy fingers on the back of my neck," Daemon stopped to take a deep breath, then continued, "Kevin can say that it's the drinking, but I know it's something more than a dream, hallucination or a guilty conscience." He stopped talking and turned my face to him. Resting his forehead on mine he went on, "And please don't get scared, but I have this feeling, this need to protect you, as if I can't leave you alone. It's some kind of magnetic pull. Like someone sent me to you." His voice was a whisper. "I'm not crazy."

I closed my eyes and waited a moment to catch my breath from his closeness, and to steady myself from the heat in my chest so I could talk. I looked back up at him. "Sometimes, I feel that I knew you before … in another life, maybe? I feel so safe with you. I can't explain it. I know you're not crazy because if you are, then we both are."

He pulled me closer in his arms and pressed his lips to my hair, my eyes and finally the lightest touch was on my lips. "Was that okay?"

I nodded my consent and buried my head in his chest. I was so tired. There was so much that I needed to say, to ask him, but my lack of sleep was catching up to me. "Stay," I said before I fell into the first peaceful sleep I'd had in days.

I woke to the sound of icy rain pelting the window. Daemon had pulled the blanket off the back of the couch and covered us both, but a chill had fallen over the room. I was wondering if we had lost power in the night with the storm. A soft gray light glowed from the windows. It was almost dawn. I tried not to move so I wouldn't wake him. He had looked almost as tired as I was last night.

Out of the corner of my eye I saw a faint movement toward the left of the room. Holding my breath, I watched as it took form, stepping from the shadows and into the faint light of the window. It was a woman, dressed in a long white gown, with her hair piled on the top of her head. As she came into focus, I could make out her features and she resembled Mary Kelly from my dreams, but her style of dress was at least a hundred years earlier, in the Victorian style, and she walked with a grace not seen today.

As I slowly sat up on the couch, she came closer to me and held out her hand. It was pale white with a pinkish glow. It radiated warmth, not the cold that came from Aaron when he appeared to me. I felt at peace with this being, not the usual impulse to run that I felt with Aaron's ghost. I rose from the couch and reached out for her hand. Taking it in mine, I shook as it seemed to blend into my own skin.

She smiled at me, warm and welcoming. "Come with me, Lilly. I have to show you something." I let her lead me through the kitchen and onto the back porch. We watched in silence as icy rain fell in streams from the overhang, creating puddles in the driveway. She lifted my arm to her face and inspected the bandage. "Why have you injured yourself? Have you not had enough pain?" I marveled at the sound of her voice, soft and musical. I had to strain to hear it over the torrent of rain. I was so entranced that I couldn't answer her. "He is real, but lost on his way, destined to roam with the nonbelievers. Those who reject purgatory are bound to their most earthly desires ... and you are his. I'm afraid that he made a deal for immortality ... a deal that he knew nothing about."

My other hand reached for her face of its' own accord, and I suddenly found my voice. "Am I being hunted? Are there other ghosts? Are you a ghost, too?"

She dropped my hand and pointed to the horizon, her white arm disappeared into the rain-soaked dawn. "The veil is at its weakest in the dawn, or when the light of the moon is the brightest. We're not ghosts Lilly; we're lost souls … those who must find the door to the throne, the other side of the moon. We are those who feel that they must pay the price." She touched my cheek and heat radiated through me, even though the rain had sent a chill deep to my bones. "You are two of the few who can see us. The veil is weakest in the time between awake and asleep, the hour before the dawn. These lost souls are not led by the Lord. They have fallen to the low lands and were made to believe that this way will bring them home." More questions were raised within my mind. She seemed to grow fainter as the storm picked up. "There are many who walk among us, but few can see us." I had to strain to hear her over the roar of the wind. "I am the spirit guide, the way of the truth. The others will deceive you. He will take your life to try to find his way home. The two will be stronger than one." After speaking these last words, she vanished with a gust of wind.

I was freezing, suddenly soaked by rain blown in the wake of her departure. I was confused and more sure than ever that Aaron was a ghost, but what connection did this woman have to him?

Chapter 17

Daemon

The storm was raging when I woke up. I was alone, the house was cold, and the gray light of dawn peaked through the slats of the blinds. Rubbing sleep from my eyes, I sat up and scanned the room for Lilly. With no sign of her in the living room, I stood up and made my way into the kitchen. Being in this house still felt a little strange to me. Well, to tell the truth, it felt a lot strange, but I loved it. Waking up here and knowing that we were together brought me peace that I hadn't felt in a long time. Just knowing that someone needed me like I needed them was filling a void in me that I didn't even know I had until a few weeks ago. All the rage I had felt yesterday seemed to diminish just knowing that Lilly was here for me.

And where was she? The house was still unfamiliar to me, but when I reached the kitchen, I heard a voice. At first I thought that Lilly was talking to someone, but I couldn't see her. Then, I realized that the voice belonged to a man, and he was talking to no one in particular. I felt the icy-cold grip on the back of my neck, a tugging pull that formed into the grips of fingers. His breath as cold as ice when he whispered into my ear, "So, how do you like my house? I trust you find it comfortable in the arms of my wife."

I jumped and turned, half expecting to find Lilly behind me, but the room was empty.

The voice whispered in my ear again, "Did I scare you, Daemon? I didn't mean to … yet." Before I could react, the icy gust of air blew over my head and materialized in front of me, taking the form of Aaron. "Don't get too comfortable here Daemon. She isn't yours. I am going to take her home."

I backed up in to the door frame, trying my best to get out of the room. But Aaron reached out a hand and grabbed my neck again, pulling me close to him. It was cold and suddenly I couldn't breathe. Panic rose up within my chest as I tried to wiggle from his grasp.

"Do I make you nervous Daemon?" Aaron asked as a sly grin spread across his face.

I managed to nod. I tried to speak, but I the words wouldn't come. Fear and panic had choked all ability to reason from my brain. Could you have a conversation with a ghost?

"Really, I don't know what Lilly sees in you. Your brother has much more strength than you. To be able to look a man in the eye and pull the trigger, to kill, takes a certain kind of strength, don't you think? But then, you looked down the barrel of the same gun, didn't you, Daemon?"

He released me from his grip and I took a deep breath to steady myself. "How did you know that?" I asked.

He looked up and down my body, then laughed. "How do you think I know that? You learn a lot when you die." I took a quick look over my shoulder, to see if Lilly was there, but I was alone with him. "Looking for a drink, Daemon? Does Lilly know that you're a drunk?"

Without even thinking I pulled my arm back to throw a punch, but was suddenly knocked down and sliding across the room on my back. When I came to a stop, Aaron was standing over me with one knee on my chest, pinning me to the ground. Once again, all the breath left my lungs.

"I wouldn't do that if I was you. You see, if you start a fight with me, you will surely lose," Aaron said, enjoying the exchange. He rose, releasing me, and stepped back a few paces, letting me collect myself before he continued, "You being in my house is really pissing me off. But so far you haven't done much of anything." I stared at him. He must have been a large man in life. Not fat, but muscled and well-built. Obviously, he had taken good care of himself. So, you carry these traits into the afterlife. He also seemed sure of himself, cocky. I could see how he thought that he was able to stop my brother. He noticed me staring at him. "Like what you see?"

I rose from the floor and walked toward him, surprising myself. "Were you always this cocky? Lilly never told me that you were such an ass." Did I just say that? Was I calling a ghost out?

To my surprise he laughed. "Well, you have some guts. I thought you would just stand there with your mouth hanging open. Still, in life, I could have taken you."

This time I swung. My hand connected with his jaw and to my surprise he stumbled backward. You could hit a ghost! He looked at me and cold and hatred radiated from his eyes. His image seemed to fade as we stared at one another. My concentration was broken when Lilly called to me in a panic from the kitchen.

"Daemon, where are you. Daemon, something has happened," she said.

I turned for a second and when I looked back, Aaron was gone. "Lilly?" I called into the darkness, rushing toward the sound of her voice.

She was waiting for me in the kitchen, soaked to the skin from the rain and pale. She was shivering, and trying to pull the bandage from her arm. "What the hell are you doing, Lilly?"

She looked at me, her eyes wide with fear, and in that second I knew that we had both seen ghosts. It took me a while to get Lilly calmed down enough to take a shower. Then, we both fell asleep on the couch again. It seemed that we had nothing to say, and no energy to talk about it.

By ten in the morning, the rain had turned to an icy, snowy mix, and we found ourselves driving to the diner in the center of town for breakfast. In a small booth overlooking the lake, I took both her hands in mine. They were cold. "Are you okay?" I asked, looking into her eyes.

She nodded and rested her head on our entwined hands. When she looked up again, her eyes had a new intensity. "What are we dealing with, Daemon? I thought it was just Aaron, but what if there are more of them?" She took a deep breath, then continued, "Daemon, I have to tell you something. Last night, I had a vision of you, Matty, and your mother. You were in the living room playing in the floor when your father came home. He pushed you away when you ran to him. It wasn't pleasant." She stopped when she felt my body grow tense. "Anyway, last night a woman appeared and she told me things. She reminded me a lot of your mother except that she was in older style of dress and I knew that she had lived in another time."

"Tell me what she said," I said, looking down at the table.

"She told me that Aaron is a non-believer and ..." she paused, not wanting to go on. The waitress set our food down on the table in front of us and refilled our coffee. "I don't even know if I want to eat, Daemon."

I picked up my fork. "You have to eat," I said, letting the subject drop for the time being, although I knew that there was something more that she wasn't telling me. "You're too pale and I'm worried about you."

She smiled and took a bite of eggs. "I like someone worrying about me." We both ate in silence for a few seconds.

"Do you want to talk about last night?" I asked, stabbing an egg.

She shook her head and downed her coffee. "There's not much to say. I'm sorry I freaked out on you. I think the woman from last night ... spirit ... whatever ... I think she's here to help me. We have to figure out her connection to Aaron."

I watched her for a minute. She had no makeup on, and a simple pair of skinny blue jeans and a black sweater, but she had never looked more beautiful in the last two weeks since I'd known her. Her green eyes were shiny from tears, and a soft pink was coming into her cheeks. I slid out of my side of the booth, slid in next to her, and wrapped my arm around her shoulder. She instinctively snuggled into me. I suddenly had the need to know everything about her. I kissed her head and said, "Tell me about Aaron."

Chapter 18

Lilly

When Daemon told me to tell him about Aaron, it took me off guard. It felt so good to lean on him, both literally and figuratively. I didn't want to ruin the moment with talk about Aaron. "What do you mean? What do you want to know?"

He looked at the table. "I didn't mean to upset you, but I just was wondering what your relationship was like with him. Maybe it'll give us some insight on why he's coming around now."

I took his chin in my hand and turned his face to mine. "You didn't upset me, just took me off guard, is all. I'll try." I closed my eyes for a long second, running through years in my mind. When I opened them, Daemon's own eyes were intent on mine.

"I met him in my junior year of college and he was a teaching assistant, finishing up his masters in engineering. We met at an off-campus party, but I had to see him again. He was handsome, strong and determined. Not only was he brilliant with any robotics items that he designed, he could build any car you asked him to. He used to race on the track and he won a lot. By the time I was graduating we were planning the wedding. I was head over heels in love, and he was heading off to a good job with the University of Massachusetts. We got married in the park, which Kat totally hated. She thought that we were too good for such a common wedding, as she called it. She wanted me to let her plan it. She even made a joke about it at our reception. After that, Aaron was really cold to her … strangely so. It was as if something had happened that he didn't want to tell me about."

I stopped when I notice Daemon grinning. "What?"

He chuckled and said, "I agree with him there. Kat is way too pretentious."

I reached over and hit him lightly on the head, and he gave me a peck on the cheek. "Go on," he said too sweetly, prompting another swat from me.

I grew serious as I continued, "I loved him, but after we were married, I noticed things. For one, he didn't really share my faith in God anymore. To him, things only mattered if they could be proved by science. Also, he worked a lot. I spent so many nights alone that it was crazy, but I tried to tell myself that his job was important, and it was work. The financial security was key to me. I had none growing up and having him take care of me was huge."

I stopped to let the waitress clear our plates and fill our coffee. Luckily, the icy rain—early for late October—had kept the restaurant on the empty side, so we took our time. Daemon took my hand in his.

"Things were going along fairly well," I continued, "Then, I said that I wanted a baby. He was totally against and he wouldn't give me a real reason why. So, I dropped it for a while. The only thing we ever really fought about was his long work hours. Then about a year and a half before he died …" I stopped to clear my throat.

Daemon gripped my hand tighter, brushed the hair from my eyes, and said, "You don't have to go on. It was unfeeling of me to ask."

I sighed. "No, I need to. I think the next part is the important part. A year and a half before he died, he started talking about ancient Druid and Celtic beliefs, the moon, and the significance of numbers. He said that he felt that the moon controlled all the power on earth, and that the Celts called "her" Morgana and worshiped her for her power. It was stuff that was really out there to me. That's when he started giving significance to numbers, like seventeen was a number associated with the visible cycles of the moon and on that day many influential and monumental events would take place. Then, I started to think he needed help. He wanted me to worship the moon with him, but it really creped me out. The look in his eyes was like he was possessed. He was searching for something."

I looked at Daemon to see how he was taking this, and he seemed to be in pensive thought, stroking the back of my hand.

"In fact the night he died," I said, "we were having dinner with his boss and he told me that he was going to ask for a leave of absence so that we could go to Europe and better research his theories and the Celtics. I told him that he was scaring me and that he was nuts. We fought and I threw the bottle of wine at him. He went out to get more … and you know the rest." When I finished, tears were flowing freely down my face. "I truly loved him, Daemon. I felt responsible for his death for a long time after. If I hadn't fought with him, doubted him, and maybe went about it in another way, he wouldn't have left the house that night. Why did I dismiss his beliefs?" Suddenly, I was in Daemon's arms and my tears were soaking the front of his shirt.

He whispered to me as he stroked my back, "It's okay, Lilly. You are in no way responsible for what happened to him. In my professional opinion, he would have eventually got into some trouble, anyway. The way he confronted a man with a loaded gun shows that he had some kind of mental disturbance going on." He paused, then added, "He knew that you loved him."

For some reason that made me cry harder. "But Daemon, now we have both seen him. Now we know that things aren't always as they seem … that the supernatural does exist. That much, he was right about." I looked up into his eyes, "And I am starting to have feelings for you. Is that not a betrayal?"

He kissed me tenderly on the lips. "It's not a betrayal. It's being human. Humans need to be together. We need companionship to survive. Something has brought us together for a reason." He looked at me intently. "You know, I've never believed in the traditional sense, either ... that there is God and Heaven and Hell ... but I always had faith that there was something more. We can't doubt him for his beliefs. He believed the only way that he could, in a ancient way, but he had some faith. You know those beliefs predated Christianity by centuries."

I nestled closer to him, ignoring the stares from the other patrons that my crying jag had brought on. "Well, what brought us together, then? Why? Because right now I feel like I never want to leave your arms."

He chuckled and said, "That's fine with me." Then, he gave me another peck on the top of my head. "You can stay in my arms forever." I noticed that he didn't answer my question. He started to pull away and put some money on the table. "Let's get going. The waitress is starting to stare us down." I let him help me into my coat and lead me to the door. He ran through the icy rain to open the passenger side door for me, and helped me in with a quick kiss. When he got in the driver's seat, he shook the icy drops of rain from his hair, leaving it in total disarray, but he never looked sexier. "I think we need to go visit my mom."

Right then, I would have gone anywhere with him, but out of the corner of my eye, I saw a shadow at the back of the car, making me shiver. It was certainly a man, but in the second that it took me to turn my head, he was gone. I looked at my lap, knowing that it was Aaron. I spoke so low that I hoped Daemon didn't hear me. "I feel like we are running *to* ghosts, instead of away from them."

Chapter 19

Daemon

I had heard Lilly's cryptic comment under her breath, but chose to ignore it. If the truth was told, this whole situation was making me as nervous as hell. It was one thing to admit that there were ghosts, but it was another to figure out ways to find them ... not that we needed any help with that. They had already found us. The question was, why *had* they found us? There always had to be a reason.

I drove toward the facility with my left hand on the wheel, and the other holding Lilly's hand. I felt that if I let her go, I would lose hold of her ... and myself. The need to protect her was becoming stronger, morphing into something else. Listening to her talk about her relationship with Aaron, however vague she was, had struck a chord with me. Her pain was deeper than the murder. It had started years before. She just hasn't realized it yet.

"Why are we going to visit your mom?" Her sudden question snapped me from my thoughts.

"I haven't checked on her in a couple of days. Plus, I wanted to see how she reacts to you for myself," I said. "Don't be mad, but I think there's a connection to her and the spirit woman you saw this morning."

She pursed her lips at me. "I'm not mad. I was kind of thinking that myself, but it sounded too out there. What I'm afraid of is the fact that we probably shouldn't be seen together there."

"Is it really any business of theirs?" I asked, concentrating on the road as I spoke. "You're free, white and over twenty-one."

She made a strange face at me. "Nice, Daemon," she said sarcastically, laughing. "That was real politically correct."

I laughed. "No really, Lilly. You're an employee there, but they can't dictate what you do in your personal life. The only one who has any valid claim to be upset about it is Kat … and that's a long shot." She looked out the window, pretending to be preoccupied with the icy road. "Are you mad that I said that?" I asked.

She was quiet for a long minute. "No. I used to think that I understood Kat's motives, but now I'm not so sure. I used to think she was truly looking out for my best interests, but truthfully, there's no one else that I could have shared this insanity with." She moved closer to me on the seat and put her hand on my leg. In that instant, I knew that I never wanted to leave her side. "So, I bared some of my soul," she said, changing the subject. "Now, it's your turn. Tell me about you and Matty."

Her question took me off guard. "Your dream was pretty much on the money. It's scary on how true it was." I glanced at her sideways. "This road is real icy. Doesn't this town ever end? We better make sure we leave for your house before the roads get any worse." It was a blatant dodge of the question. I kind of felt bad when I saw the look on her face, but I was in no mood to go into it right now. I pulled into the parking lot of the facility and turned the engine off. Then, I leaned back in the seat and closed my eyes, letting the sound of the icy rain against the Volvo's roof relax me. I felt her hand on my leg … the warmth it radiated. "It wasn't pretty, Mattie and me," I began. "I got out, left town. My mom was the only thing that brought me back here, and you're the only reason why I'm staying now."

Lilly was quiet, she looked at me with a knowing look in her eyes. "I didn't mean to pry," she whispered.

I reached up and gently placed my hand on the back of her neck, feeling the softness of her amber colored hair, and pulled her to me. "You don't need to be sorry," I said, stroking her hair as she rested her head on my chest.

She laughed as she pressed her lips to mine. "I'm not."

No one paid us any mind as we walked hand in hand down the hallway to my mother's room. It was Sunday and the facility was quiet with the early afternoon sounds of lunch trays being served. My mother's room was dark and warm. She was sleeping in the reclining chair by the window. I sat on the edge of the bed and Lilly went over to draw back the curtains. "I think it's turning back to regular rain. It felt a little warmer when we were walking in."

"I told those damned fools that it would ... all that grumbling about the horses slipping ..." Mom said, abruptly breaking the silence. We both jumped at the sound of her voice. Lilly recovered faster.

"Mrs. Kelly, we didn't mean to wake you," Lilly said, concerned.

She coughed and grunted. "Nonsense! Did you think that I was going sleep all day? Those dresses are not going to make themselves."

Lilly and I exchanged smiles before I got up and knelled down next to my mother, taking her hand. "Hi, Mom. I heard you met Lilly earlier this week?"

She smiled and replied, "Yes, the lilies ... did you ever get them back from Matty? He never took care of things right."

I glanced over at Lilly with a nervous look, but she seemed to be taking the comment in stride. The professionalism in her was taking over. "It's okay, Mrs. Kelly," Lilly said, smiling. "I made it back all right." Then, she turned to smile at me. I was amazed by her composure.

It also amazed me how my mother went in and out of reality. Her next comment took me off guard. "Did you kids make it here all right? The aides were talking about how bad the roads were. Daemon, are you ever going to make an honest woman of this lovely lady here?"

I seized the lucid moment she was having. "Mom, why do you keep asking about bringing Matty lilies? Do you know where he is?"

She squinted at the window, as if she was trying to make something out the window in the rain come into focus. She didn't even hear me. Her eyes were focused only on Lilly. "Lilly, did Aunt Rita come see you?" she asked. "She was here last week and she said she would pop in on you. Was she wearing that gorgeous dress? So inappropriate for this time of year, don't you think?"

I watched as Lilly's face turned white, and barely made it to her in time to catch her before she hit the floor as she fainted. I slid down onto the floor with her, brushed away the beads of sweat on her face, and watched her eyelids flutter. "Lilly, are you okay? Come back to me, hon."

She blinked a few times and looked at me, confused and scared. "Daemon, the woman from last night ... it was Aunt Rita. I don't know how I know, but I just know it." She tried to get up, but I held her tightly as I checked her pulse. Her heart was racing.

"Lilly, calm down," I said. "Just sit with me for a minute. I don't want you to start hyperventilating." I thought for a moment, then asked, "How do you know? I mean ... my mom doesn't know what she's saying. You know that, right?"

I let her slide from my lap, but held onto her. She dropped her head to her hands, letting the tears flow. When she raised her head to look at me, her face was so pale that it scared me, but her eyes were intense.

"She was dressed in white organza," Lilly replied. "Like I told you earlier, she looked just like your mom ... only younger."

I wiped a tear away from her cheek as it slid down her face. "Lilly, my mom's Aunt Rita is the only 'Aunt Rita' I

Becca Boucher

can think of, and she was old when I was young. I mean, she must have been like ninety when she died ... and that was in the early eighties."

She shook her head. "Then, it makes sense," Lilly reasoned. "The dress was in a style from long ago—Victorian, I think—but it could have been from the late twenties or early thirties. She said that we were closest to the spirit world in the space between awake and asleep, near dawn. If that's the case, then your mom could be extremely sensitive to that veil. She could see Aunt Rita any time she wishes."

I put my hand to her cheek. "Lilly, I know how much you want to believe this ..."

"No Daemon," she said, cutting me off. "It's real! I thought you were on board with this! Your mom has lucid moments. Her Alzheimer's is not as advanced as you thought, or maybe the medicine is working, but she can see the spirit guide, too. I think she is the one telling her about the lilies. And the lilies aren't flowers ... she's talking about me!"

I listened to what she was saying. If I didn't believe her, it would push her away. I would be someone else abandoning her. But the opposite—if it were true—meant that we were dealing with more than what we had originally thought ... something much bigger.

I didn't have time to voice my thoughts, though, when my mother's voice suddenly interrupted us, coming from the chair, upset and angry. "What do you want from us? I talked to you yesterday."

I looked up to see Kat in the doorway. "Well, isn't this cozy. One of the aides said that Mrs. Kelly had visitors, and then someone was saying that they heard some kind of commotion going on down here. Since I was already up here making my lunch rounds, I thought I would stop in." The look on her face was anything but friendly.

Lilly and I got up from the floor and I went over and took my mom's hand. "It's okay, Mom. I think she's here to see Lilly, not you." It was anything but okay. Lilly looked at me, and there were tears in her eyes.

The look on Kat's face turned venomous as she looked at me. "What did you do to her? I knew this would happen! You're no good for her!" Her voice was rising and my mother's hand started to shake in her lap.

I stood and started toward Kat. "Look here, you need to stay out of our business. It doesn't concern you ..."

Lilly jumped between us. "Kat, I think we should take this out into the hall. Go on out and I'll meet you out there." Kat left with a huff and Lilly crossed the room and knelt in front of my mom. "Mary, it's okay. I am okay. Daemon is going to stay right here with you while I go into the hallway to talk to Kat. I'll be right back, okay?" She leaned in and kissed my mom on the cheek, and Mom reached for her hand. "Okay, Lilly. We'll watch the baby." Lilly rose to her feet, patted my hand and walked from the room. It was at that moment that I knew that I loved her.

Chapter 20

Lilly

"*What the hell, Kat?*" I turned on her as soon as we were out in the hallway. "You keep jumping in conversations that you know nothing about, and now you've scared Mary half to death! That was real professional, by the way."

Kat grabbed the hand rail that ran along the wall and hung her head. I could see her fingers clench the wood, trying to calm down. When she turned to face me I was surprised to see tears on her face. "I just don't understand how you can be with him. You were sitting there on the floor ... in his lap ... and it just killed me. How can you separate the two?"

I took a tentative step toward her. "He didn't pull the trigger, Kat," I said. "He didn't even know what was happing. If you only gave him a chance, you would see that he's nothing like his brother."

She shook her head. "How can you say that? Do you know anything about him? How do you know that one day you won't wake up with a gun to your head?"

I put my hands on her shoulders and she didn't move away from me. "Kat, there is so much going on right now and Daemon ... he's good, Kat. He knows the pain to lose family, to lose your grip on things. He knows how much it hurts."

She met my eyes. "And I don't?"

"No, Kat. You don't know what it feels like to have your world shattered, your love stolen." I measured my next words very carefully. "I've seen Aaron, Kat. He ... he is ... stuck between this world and the next. He comes to me in the night and shows me things. I'm scared, Kat, and Daemon has seen him, too."

She took a step away from me. Her close cut black hair and her ever so chick nails was the picture of the perfect woman. What did she know about loss? She always gets everything she wants. Her voice was low when she spoke. "You mean, like a ghost? Are you crazy, Lilly? You think some half-baked story about seeing Aaron's ghost is funny? Of course he would say he saw him, too, to get close to you! I loved him, too, Lilly! So don't fricken play me for a fool!"

My stomach flipped, unable to believe what I was hearing. "Loved who, Kat?"

She shook again as she spoke. "Aaron. I should have been the one with him, not you. I was so jealous when he asked you to marry him ... I mean ... I was kind of glad after he wanted to get married in the park and all ... but I was much better suited for the academic life than you are! Do you know that the week before he asked you out, when we met him at the campus book store, I slept with him? That whole year, he was with me when he wasn't with you. He just couldn't stand that I had my own goals." She walked closer to me as I listened in disbelief. The woman who had everything couldn't let me have the man that I loved. "I promised him that I would never tell you, but this negates all of that, Lilly. He confided in me the month before he died that he was seeing someone else. I made him stay with you, Lilly, because if he wasn't with you, then it should have been me. I was going to fix it, and for you to disrespect his memory like this with that white-trash brother of a killer is inexcusable. It just confirms that I was better for him than you."

My knees shook, I felt like I was going to faint again. "Kat, why are you doing this to me?" My voice was barely a whisper.

Becca Boucher

She ignored me, hell bent on getting everything out. "You know why he asked you out? He wanted a puppet, Lilly. He knew that you would sit back and let him run the show. I would have talked him out of that park wedding, and I would have run right off to Scotland."

I backed away from her, my head was ringing. I needed to get out. Her words were slicing me in the heart like no knife ever could.

It was then that I felt Daemon's arms around me, turning me into his chest. "I think you need to leave, Kat. There's no point for you to bring this up right now. If you ever come near her again, I'll call the police." A nurse started down the hall. The raised voices were attracting attention.

"Really Daemon, I think you're the one that needs to stay away from her," Kat said as venom pour from her lips.

I had to hold Daemon back, clinging to his arm. Kat stormed down the hall and Daemon guided me back into his mother's room. I sat on the edge of the bed and took his mom's hand. I looked at him, at a loss for words. At that moment, all that I wanted was to be in his arms.

Ten minutes later, I was sitting in the passenger side of my Volvo waiting for Daemon to come out of the facility. In my lap laid the framed picture of Mary's Aunt Rita. Daemon had placed it in my hands as I fled from the room. I was shaking. Kat's words were running through my head mixed with images of guardian angels and spirit guides.

As I laid my head back in my seat, the vibration in my pocket alerted me to the existence of my phone. It was a text from Daemon. *Be right out,* it said. A small smile escaped my lips. As I held the phone, gazing at the message, a thought came over me.

I opened the Web browser and typed in "spirit guides" on the Goggle page. I hoped that something would come up, but I was not prepared for over 10,000 hits. I scrolled down and picked a random entry from the encyclopedia Britannica, *an angel or demon, is respectively any benevolent or malevolent spiritual being that mediates between the transcendent and temporal realms.*

I went back to the search page and clicked further down, hoping to find something which proved their existence. What I found next struck a chord with me. *In traditional belief, a* **ghost** *is the soul or spirit of a deceased person or animal that can appear, in visible form or other manifestation, to the living. Descriptions of the apparition of ghosts vary widely: The mode of manifestation can range from an invisible presence to translucent or wispy shapes, to realistic, life-like visions."* Whoever the author of the Wikipedia entry was seemed to believe. He went on to say that all cultures had varying beliefs in the afterlife and death.

I jumped a mile when my research was interrupted by Daemon bounding into the driver's seat. "Sorry, Lilly. I didn't mean to scare you. What are you looking at?"

I blushed as I snapped my phone shut. "Nothing. I was just waiting for you."

He looked at me a minute, but let it pass. His eyes were so intense that he took my hand before he spoke. "Lilly," he began hesitantly, "I don't think that Kat meant anything that she said back there. She just feels hurt and confused, is all."

"I know, Daemon," I said, cutting him off. "I knew about them before I accepted the first date with him. He told me, but I had no idea that she still had feelings for him … that things were still going on …"

He noticed my floundering thoughts and jumped in. "Just, please don't let her change how we're connecting. Back there … the way you were with my mom, how you have accepted me these past few weeks, the more time I spend with you…" he said, but stopped to look down.

Even though I was slightly afraid of what he was going to say, I needed to hear it. I reached over and turned his head toward me. "It's okay, D. Go on … please."

He rested his hand on my cheek and closed his eyes for a long second, then looked at me so tenderly. "I love you."

Tears started to flow down my cheeks and before I knew what he was doing, he pulled me across the seats and onto his lap. His hands were in my hair, my eyes closed as I pressed my lips to his. I felt his sharp intake of breath as I parted my lips to invite a longer kiss. He softly bit my bottom lip and moved his hand down my stomach and under my shirt, running his hand along the soft skin of my back.

At that moment, I was so content that I never wanted to leave his arms or for his lips to leave mine. It had been so long since anyone had loved me, maybe since months before Aaron had died. I didn't want to stop kissing him, pulling him tighter to me. The strong muscles of his arms, and the firmness of his chest pressed against mine. I was trying to pull his sweatshirt up over his head when he stopped me.

"Don't you think we better move along? This might not be the optimal location to … umm …" He gently wiped at the tears on my face. "Are you sure you're okay with this?"

I slid back over to my seat and pulled my shirt down. Nodding my head, I managed to find my voice. "I need you, Daemon. We're in this together. I need you in my life," then my voice was merely a whisper, "And I want you, Daemon." It was the closest that I could come to I love you at the moment, but from the look in his eyes, it would do.

Chapter 21

Daemon

I felt a certain sense of elation as I backed out of the parking space and left the facility. I had told Lilly how I felt, and she was still here, sitting next to me with her hand tightly in mine. True, she hadn't told me that she loved me back, but her response meant just as much. I loved hearing her say that she needed me. I looked over at her from the corner of my eye and saw that she was nodding off. It had been a long day for her, after a sleepless night. We had learned so much, but what we learned had raised so many more questions. I chuckled, whispering, "Go to sleep, hon. I'll wake you when we get home."

She looked at me, smiling sleepily. "Can we go to your house?"

She closed her eyes as I brought her hand to my lips. "I'll take you anywhere you want to go, Lilly. Do you need to stop at your house for anything first?"

She laughed and replied, "No, I'll just steal a T-shirt from you for tonight. We can go to my house tomorrow." We drove in silence for a few minutes as the radio softly played one of the slower songs of *Breaking Benjamin*.

"I didn't know you were a rock fan," I teased her, before noticing that she was now fully asleep. The blue glow from the dial illuminated her features as I drove. She looked peaceful in her sleep, all worry was gone from her face and she looked younger. I reached over to brush the hair back from her cheek and felt a sting of longing. The rain that had fallen most of the day had stopped. In the dusk, I could see

Becca Boucher

the bare branches of the trees, adding to the eeriness of Halloween, which was in two weeks. So much had changed since the beginning of October. Now, I could no longer imagine my world without Lilly, without her, life would be as empty as the branches of the tress we drove under.

I think tonight called for a case of beer and a bottle of wine. I pulled into the package store in the center of town. Lilly stirred as I shut off the car. "Everything okay?" she asked, taking in her surroundings. Suddenly, she grew quiet. Damn, what if this was *the* store. How could I be so stupid? She noticed the look on my face and rushed to reassure me. "I'm okay, just surprised me that we're stopping here."

I turned in my seat to face her. "Is it okay? I thought you might like some wine."

She looked at me. "It's fine. You don't have to over analyze everything you do. A package store is not going to bring me to tears. Go. I'm staying in the car."

I kissed her quickly on the forehead and jumped from the car. The day had been cold for October. It had started with icy rain, but as I opened the door to the store I was met with a blast of icy air. They must have not turned their heat on yet. I made my way to the back of the store and pulled a case of beer from the freezer. Then, I walked up a few rows until I found the wine and picked out a bottle of *Pinot Grigio* for Lilly. When I got to the front of the store I held the bottle of wine to the window for her approval. She laughed and waved me toward the counter.

The store had been empty when I entered, now there was one other couple standing at the counter. As I stood behind them, a blast of cold air hit my neck, followed by the feeling of gripping fingers pulling me back. *Not now,* I thought to myself. I knew what was happening even before I spun around to find no one behind me. Then, I heard the menacing words as clear as day, close to my ear, "You left her alone. Not smart, Daemon." Spinning around, I lost my grip on the bottle, but caught it before it hit the ground.

The couple at the counter gave me a dirty look as they left the store. Soft laughter echoed in my ear behind me. The clerk waved me up, "You okay?"

I glanced toward the large plate glass window, did Lilly see what happened? She was sitting in the car staring right at me, as if she knew exactly what was going on. I took one step toward the counter before I was pulled back by the collar of my shirt so hard that I gasped for air. This time the bottle slipped again, but it didn't break when it hit the floor. In fact, it bounced back up into my hand just as I was pushed toward the counter.

The clerk stared at me before he spoke. "I shouldn't sell to you if you're already drunk, man. Are you sure you're okay?"

I cleared my throat, trying to come up with something besides "my girlfriend's dead husband is trying to get my attention." "Yeah," I said instead. "It's just really cold in here. I got a chill, trying to shake it off." He took the wine and beer from me to ring it up.

"Cold? I turned the heat on this afternoon. The other people were just saying that it was too warm. You sure you're okay? I can call someone for you, if you like."

Glancing out the window at Lilly, I answered him with a sneer, "My girlfriend is in the car. She'll drive."

He shook his head and took my money. I turned from the counter to walk to the door when it felt as if I had ran into a brick wall. The force of it pushed me to the ground and took all the breath from my lungs. I tried to stand, but my feet slipped on the floor. When I regained my footing, I ran to the door with the clerk yelling at my back, "You're lucky I'm not calling the police, freaking drug addicts!"

I pushed the door open and found Lilly running up the sidewalk toward me. "What the hell is going on? Are you okay?"

I took her elbow and guided her back to the car. "Get in the car. It was Aaron."

Becca Boucher

Her face turned white. "Aaron? But it's daytime! Five o'clock in the afternoon."

We got in the car and I slammed the button for the door locks. "We can't talk about it now. If we don't get out of here the clerk is going to call the cops, but Aaron was getting physical with me in the store."

She started to shake and I took her hand. "It's going to be okay. As soon as we get home, we're going to research this. I'm not leaving you alone."

As I spoke I put the car in reverse and started to back up, just when Lilly screamed. I saw him just as she did, standing at the rear of the car on the passenger side. He was holding onto the back of the car, keeping it in place. He was dressed in black and as pale as the moon, but visible none the less. He laughed, cold and hard, different from the first time I had seen him. He spoke and even though all the windows in the car were up, we could hear him as plain as day. "Did you ask him about his name yet, Lilly? You can come home with me, Lilly. I'll take you home."

Lilly screamed and sobbed. It was a terrifying sound that put me into action. I could see the clerk in front of me as he held the phone to his ear. I could hear sirens in the distance.

"What does he want from me?" Lilly asked with her head in her hands, pulling at her hair. That did it. I put the car back in reverse and hit the gas. I felt a thump as I spun the tires and went up over the curb. Could you run over a ghost? All of a sudden I felt his hands on my neck pulling me over the seat into the back.

I yelled at Lilly to take the wheel. She somehow slid over and got behind the wheel as I put my elbow into Aaron's chest with all my force. It was like hitting stone. Lilly fishtailed out of the parking lot and took the first left, headed back to where we had come from. I was kicking at Aaron, grasping for anything I could. Lilly was screaming for me, screaming for Aaron, and crying so hard that the car went up on the sidewalk.

"Lilly! Try and calm down," I yelled as my foot connected with Aaron's face and the force flung the door open. At the same time, I knew that every bone in my foot was broken. "Lilly take the next right!" I struggled to sit up. Alone in the back seat, I could hear the police cars. "Lilly, the next road on the left is a dirt road! Take it and pull behind that grove of trees."

She stopped and I climbed back over the seat and turned the car off. I crouched down in the seat and pulled her down with me as the sirens grew faint in the distance. We sat like that until it was pitch black, until her tears had soaked my shirt, and the clouds had cleared enough for the stars to come out. Neither one of us said a word.

Later, I sat up and looked out the window. It had been a while since the sirens had faded in the distance. It was pitch black now and quiet. Lilly had fallen asleep as I kept vigil for police cars or for Aaron to return.

The night was getting colder. In the back of my mind, I remembered a weather forecast from earlier in the week saying that the first frost of the year was expected. It made no sense, but we had frozen rain earlier in the day. I laughed without humor. Weathermen were nothing but fortune tellers. I fumbled for my watch and struggled to see the time … eight at night … we were certainly in the clear to make our way home.

I shook Lilly and she woke with a start. "It's okay," I said reassuring her. "There's no sign of anyone, living or dead."

She looked at me with faint disbelief in her eyes. "Making jokes of this? I don't see anything funny about the situation." I was starting to defend myself when she hugged me. "Sorry. You startled me when you woke me up." Then, she noticed me wince. "Your foot?" I shifted my weight and nodded. "Yeah. You're going to have to drive home. I feel like I kicked a brick wall. From the way it's swelling, I think it might be broken."

Lilly sat up in the driver's seat and looked out the window. She was shaking as she started the car. "Are you okay?"

She put a lot of effort into steadying her voice. "No, but I can make it home. When we get to your house, I'll lose it." The tires spun a little as she accelerated, then she slammed down on the gas as we hit the road.

When we pulled into my driveway, Kevin was home. A welcoming glow streamed from the windows and the smell of fresh bread hit us as I opened the back door. Kevin was standing in the kitchen when we walked in, stirring something in a pot that was simmering on the stove. "Well, it's about time someone else showed up! You guys hungry? I assumed that you weren't alone, dude. I heard two doors close. There's plenty of food." He stopped talking as he turned and looked at us. "What the hell happened to you two?"

I was standing just inside the kitchen door, leaning on Lilly's shoulder. My shirt was un tucked and my sweatshirt was hanging off the arm that wasn't draped around Lilly. I was desperately trying to keep my weight off my right foot, and I was sure that my coloring was the same as Lilly. Her face had taken on a strange pallor, a combination of white and a sickish gray. Her eyes were rimmed with red and it was evident she had been crying. We must have looked as if we had been in a dog fight.

Kevin rushed over, leaving the spaghetti sauce bubbling on the stove. He took the majority of my weight off Lilly and pulled out a chair from the table. "Damn it, D. What the hell happened to your foot?"

I ignored him, sinking into the chair. Lilly pulled out the chair next to me and plopped down. She leaned over and buried her head in my shoulder. I could feel her heart shudder in her chest.

"Can someone please tell me what the hell is going on here?," Kevin demanded. "I really would like to know why you two look like you were in a fight. Let me see that foot, Daemon."

I laughed without humor, not knowing where to start. The situation was just too crazy for words. "Before or after we hid out from the police? Or maybe when I was being attacked by Aaron in the package store? Or when the clerk thought I was a druggie and Lilly was trying to crawl over me to the driver's seat? Or maybe when I kicked a solid-brick ghost out of the car and broke my foot? You really had to be there, Kev!"

Lilly lifted her head up, aware that I was becoming irrational. "Calm down, Daemon," she said. She ran her hands through her hair, smoothed it down, as the panic in her eyes softened. Some sort of strange acceptance spread over her features. "We saw Aaron, but it was different this time. He was physical, looking for a fight. He attacked Daemon in broad daylight ... in public. He's so different now than he was in life." She seemed to be talking more to herself than us.

Kevin walked back over to the stove and shut the sauce off. He braced himself against the counter and looked out the window over the sink. The rain had stopped and the moon was bright enough to see the trees at the back of the driveway. He turned around to face us, uncertain. "I don't know if I can handle this. It was different when you two said that he was like a strange figure in the night, but telling me he was physical with you ... that you fought him? That's some messed up shit. It kind of goes against everything I believe in, man. Ghosts can't be real man."

I winced. I don't know if it was from the pain in my foot, or if it was because his words were giving voice to all that I was feeling. Even living through it, you couldn't help but question what was happening. I glanced down at my foot and he said, "Let me take a look at your foot. I just have to go to the truck and get my bag." As he pushed away from the sink, I took Lilly's hand. "Could you grab the stuff from the package store out of Lilly's car while you're out there?"

He shook his head before he answered, "That depends, you got beer?"

Halfway through the case of beer, we determined that my foot wasn't broken. It was badly bruised and sore, but still useable. Kevin wrapped it in an ace bandage and made me put ice on it. Lilly was sipping at her wine quietly on the couch, and wasn't even through the first glass. I slid down on the couch beside her and asked, "Are you okay?"

She glanced up at me, twirling the glass of wine in her hand. Her gaze was both pensive and troubled. "What if Kevin's right? What if we're both crazy?"

Kevin looked up as he cracked open his beer. "I never said you were crazy," he corrected. "Just because I never saw a ghost before, doesn't mean that I think you're crazy. I just can't wrap my mind around it."

I pulled her to me and she rested her hand on my knee. At that simple touch, my body burned with desire … and my soul burned with an intense drive to protect her. She looked back and forth between Kevin and me. At that moment I knew we weren't crazy at all. "We obviously saw something. Hell, my foot felt something. Even if it went right through him and I kicked the car door, I still was defending myself … I felt him."

Lilly nodded. Fixing her gaze on Kevin, she said with intensity, "I never believed it either, until I lived it … until the dreams haunted my every night, coming more and more alive until he stepped out of them … until D's mother told me things she possibly couldn't know … until I felt his icy touch on my skin." She took my hand, winding her fingers through mine. Then, she placed her glass of wine on the floor. Every move seem filled with intent. She was tired. I could feel it in her touch.

Kevin checked his watch. "Well, peeps, I have to be at work at five. Public service waits for no man. I'm turning in." He stepped over to Lilly, and touched her head, like I had seen him do millions of times before with his kid sister. "We'll figure this out. I never meant to make you feel like that."

She smiled a sad smile. "It's okay, Kevin. We shouldn't drag you into this."

Kevin laughed. "Like you could keep me away!" Then, he yelled over his shoulder as he retreated up the stairs, "Behave you two!"

Becca Boucher

Chapter 22

Lilly

As we watched Kevin make his way up the stairs, I was overly aware of how close Daemon was to me. The way our legs rested against each other, the casual way my hand lingered on his knee. The events of the day and the effects of the wine clouded my mind. I was tired. The only thing I knew with certainty was that I wouldn't have to be alone tonight. I wouldn't have to fear the dark. I wouldn't have to face this alone, but what was I facing? I was suddenly aware of Daemon's hand lightly tracing circles on my neck. I leaned into him. "I need a shower. Do you have one of those?"

He chuckled, then said, "I think I remember a room upstairs that might fit the bill. Come on, I'll get you settled."

I watched him as he rose from the couch and turned off the lights in the den. He turned to me and held out his hand. I took it as I rose and used the warmth to steady my nerves. "How's your foot?"

"I think I'll live. I won't be taking you hiking any time soon, but it feels better already," he said, making a little attempt to dance a jig, but winced as his foot hit the ground. I raised an eyebrow at him and he blushed. "I'll show you the bathroom and then my room. I think I'll crash down here on the couch tonight and give you your space."

I stopped in my tracks at the bottom of the stairs. There was no way I was sleeping alone tonight, but I didn't know how to say as much without sounding desperate. I fought the sudden sting of tears in my eyes and turned away.

"Lilly, what's wrong?" he asked, concerned.

When I turned to face him, he looked so much older than when I first met him two weeks ago. The events of the day had certainly taken a toll on us both, but his gorgeous eyes were burning right through me. "I don't want to be alone. Not tonight. Please, Daemon, come with me." He kissed the top of my head and pulled me by the hand silently up the stairs.

After eliciting a promise from him that he would stay in his room, I went to the bathroom. It was cleaner than I expected it would be for two young bachelors. Aside from the hair left in the sink and the clothes on the floor, it was relatively tidy. I laid the clean towels and the large T-shirt I borrowed from Daemon on the hamper and turned to the mirror. I looked like hell. Lack of sleep from the night before, the confrontation at the nursing home with Kat, and the run-in with Aaron had taken its toll. My clothes looked like I had slept in them, and my hair was tangled around my face. No wonder Daemon offered to say on the couch.

I let the shower run as I undressed and felt a twinge of familiar shame when I took my sweater off and saw the bandage on my arm. I pulled the tape and took off the gauze. It looked better since Daemon had wrapped it, but it was definitely the deepest that I had ever cut myself. I cursed Aaron under my breath, and slipped into the hot water.

It was like heaven to my tired muscles and I let it rain down on me for what seemed like forever. The only soap I could find was a bar of Ivory on the rim above the shower, and it brought back memories of my mom's house. The way life used to be. If anyone could fall asleep in the shower, it would have been me that night. As I turned off the water, I heard a soft knock on the door.

"You okay in there, Lil? Or did you want to use all the hot water up on me?" he joked.

I wiped my eyes on the towel and cracked open the door. "I'll be right out, worry wart." Daemon poked me through the crack. As I pulled his soft T-shirt over my head, I wondered how I could feel so happy, when hell—in the form of Aaron—was knocking at my door.

The twenty minutes that Daemon was in the shower had to be the longest twenty minutes of my life. I waited with bated breath for him to come back in the door, and alternated that with the fear that he would be coming back in the door. When he finally stepped in and closed the door behind him, all my trepidation vanished. He was still wet. Small drops of water clung to his bangs and his bare, muscular chest was damp. He looked at me sitting in the middle of his bed, with my knees pulled into my chest, and smiled. He sat at the foot and looked at me intently. I cleared my throat and forced myself to sound more confident than I was. "How is your foot?"

He looked down and back up at me. "How many times are you going to ask me that tonight? I think the warm water—what was left of it, anyway—helped relax it. It feels at least fifty percent better." He grinned at me, waiting for a reply to his smartass comments.

Instead, I inched closer to him and put my head on his shoulder, taking in the warmth of his body and the clean smell of soap on his skin. His arm encircled my shoulders, pulling me close. I sighed. "How can I feel so happy, when everything is coming apart around me? How can I still want you so badly ... when he is trying to keep us apart?"

His answer was to tilt my head up and place his lips softly on mine. The clock on his nightstand was the only sound in the room. Even our hearts seemed to be still. My lips parted to take him in, and we leaned back against the pillows. I tangled myself up in his arms and he pulled back to look at me.

"You deserve to be happy," he said, then continued, "Whatever misguided emotions lurk in the soul of that ghost, you shouldn't be made to pay for his mistakes."

I appreciated the way Daemon resisted saying his name. I didn't want anything to take me out of this moment. The only thing I wanted to think of was being in Daemon's arms. I never wanted to leave this room. I closed my eyes and pulled him closer to me, wanting and needing his lips on mine. Whatever happened tomorrow could happen, but right now, this moment was about us. I felt his hand on my back, his lips on my neck and the soft sighs that escaped him only caused me to fall deeper into his embrace. When I opened my eyes, he was looking at me with so much emotion that it melted my heart. There was so much love in that single glance, more than words could express in a lifetime. I wrapped my legs around him and time ceased to exist.

The next morning, I was suddenly aware of the room getting lighter. I was tangled in the sheets, but blissfully rested. I hadn't slept that good in over a year. My hand traveled over the rumpled sheets and met the strong curve of Daemon's back. I could tell by the even breaths he took that he was still sleeping deeply. I rolled over, rested my head against his shoulder, and closed my eyes again, letting my mind run over yesterday's events. Even though I didn't want to think about Aaron and the encounter with Kat, I needed to. Kat would be the easier one to figure out. Whatever she said had been motivated by jealousy and grief. Aaron had told me about their encounter when we first started dating, but the fact she still harbored feelings for him was a little bit of a surprise. I had always known of the envious and diabolical Kat that lingered beneath the surface, but I always choose to concentrate on her good points. Now, I didn't know if I could ever go back to being her friend again.

Then, there was Aaron. He was more real than any ghost in any movie, shattering all my preconceived notions of the "afterlife." There was no doubt in my mind that he was real and whatever strange obsession that had held him hostage in the last year of his life was still motivating him ... as well as his need to "protect" me. The key was to figure out what it was. Whether it had to do with the Celtic legends he had become obsessed with, or something else, I had no clue. All of it was making my mind, and heart, race.

Daemon began to stir next to me and I found myself smiling with anticipation. It was a new day in a new love … and I was feeling eager to meet it. I heard my phone ring in my purse across the room. Daemon rolled over and nuzzled my neck. "Phone. Ringing," he said, his voice husky with sleep.

I chuckled and replied, "What day is it? I think I might have to be at work."

He laughed. "Monday. Halloween is this Saturday." The phone stopped ringing and went to voice mail.

I rolled over to face him. "I'm quitting work. Right now, I don't need the money and I don't need the hassle. I have enough insurance money left to last a year."

Daemon's eyes snapped open, "When did you decide this?"

"Right now, when the phone rang," I said. I knew it was sudden, but I was sure. "I was lying here thinking about yesterday and about us, and I don't want to spend one more day there. I need to focus on why Aaron is appearing … why he can't rest in peace. Maybe if I put it all behind me, I can love you with a clear heart and mind."

Daemon rested his forehead against mine and softly kissed my nose before he rose up on his elbow to stare in my eyes. "Are you sure about this? I have a feeling that if you quit, there's no going back … to the facility or to anything else. If we pursue this, there's no telling where it's going to lead us." He brushed a strand of hair from my face. "You just admitted that you love me," he said, as one corner of his lips curled into a sexy half smile. "There's definitely no going back from that."

I stared into his impossible-to-believe blue eyes and reached up to run my fingers through his dark hair, still damp from the shower because it was so thick. "Silly boy, I don't want to take that back. You believe me when no one else would, and you saved my heart." I flopped back down against the pillows and looked up at the ceiling. Daemon lay next to me and took my hand. We stayed there for what seemed like hours, lost in the sincerity of the moment. I was the one to break the hold. "I need to call Kat and there's no use postponing the inevitable. The sooner I resign, the better it will be."

Daemon rose from the bed and pulled on a pair of well-worn sweat pants. I couldn't help but stare as he searched for a T-shirt. He caught me checking him out and chuckled. "Why don't I give you some privacy to make that call?" he asked with his hand on the door handle. "I'll go down stairs and make us some breakfast."

Becca Boucher

Chapter 23

Daemon

I left Lilly alone in my room to call Kat and her work, then made my way to the stairs. In the morning sun, I could see the bruise on my right ankle. I had pulled the ace bandage off as soon as I got in the bathroom last night. Even though the black was spreading over my foot into a sickening shade of yellow and purple, the pain was almost gone. I walked down the stairs into the living room to find Kevin standing in front of the TV. He turned when he heard me. "We have big problems, bro. Come look at this."

I stood next to him in front of the TV and tried to focus on what the reporter on the morning news was saying. The "Breaking News" banner kept running across the bottom of the screen. They kept switching back and forth from the news room to a shot of a correctional facility swarmed with what looked like swat team members running in. Kevin turned up the sound.

"To recap, a maximum security prisoner has escaped during the night from MCI Concord. Matthew Spencer, convicted and sentenced earlier this month for the murders of two men, was found missing from his cell this morning. Routine cell checks have turned up no sign of the prisoner, and area schools and hospitals are in lockdown."

My head felt weak as my right hand balled up into a fist. Kevin placed his hand on my shoulder and pushed me to the couch. I was shaking; life was making no sense.

The TV continued to drone on. "At this time, the escaped prisoner has not been found. There was no sign of forced entry into the cell, and officials have no idea how the door could have been left open. We ask anyone with any information to contact the State Police. Do not try to approach him; he is considered to be armed and dangerous."

Kevin picked up the remote and turned the TV off. "Shit, D. How the hell did this happen? We got Lilly upstairs, how are we going to tell her? The freaking police will be knocking on the door anytime now to make sure the dick isn't here." He was pacing, and the aggravation on his face surely mimicked mine. My head dropped to my hands. I spoke to myself more than to him. I wasn't sure how I even knew it, but I was certain. "Aaron is behind this. How the hell else could he get out?" I asked, knowing full well that I sounded like a crazy man.

Kevin stopped dead in his tracks. "Aaron? The dead guy? Are you nuts, Daemon?" Kevin asked in disbelief. "Even if a dead guy can break a prisoner out of jail, why would he break out the guy who killed him, huh? Enlighten me on that one, Daemon, because that just makes no sense whatsoever!"

"What doesn't make sense?" We both turned to see Lilly coming down the stairs. My T-shirt was hanging loose on her slender frame, and her green eyes were focused intently on mine.

"Lilly … the news … something has happened," I said, afraid of what this might do to her.

She stopped at the bottom of the stairs and looked at me, her green eyes searching my face. Her voice was barely a whisper. "What, Daemon? Is it Aaron? Was Aaron here?"

I crossed the floor to her and took her hands in mine. "Matty," I began, watching her eyes grow wide. "He broke out of jail last night. It's all over the news."

Her voice broke ever so slightly. "What does this mean? I don't understand."

I had a jumble of images in my mind, images of Aaron and Matty assaulting my thoughts.

Kevin spoke, bringing me back to the present. "D thinks it's Aaron," Kevin said to Lilly. "He thinks that Aaron somehow used his ghostly powers to break Matty out of jail. All I know is that sometime soon we are going to be getting a visit for the police and we better damned well know what we're going to say."

I sat down on the stairs and pulled Lilly down next to me. Her hand trembled in mine. "Slow down, Kev," I said, rubbing Lilly's back. "They can ask all the questions they want. They can search the house, but they aren't going to find a single thing. What we have to figure out is why he's out, and how Aaron broke him out."

Kevin turned from his pacing to face me. His face was a mask of anger. "You're serious, aren't you? You're really loosing it, Daemon," Kevin said in disbelief. "You really believe that a ghost broke him out of jail? I wasn't going to argue with the two of you last night, but maybe you *are* nuts. I've humored you long enough. You're drinking again and seeing shit, aren't you? And Lilly is too lost in her own grief to not believe you!"

I started to rise off the stair when Lilly pulled me back down by the arm. She spoke, without a hint of hesitation. "Kevin, I was the one who dragged Daemon into this," Lilly softly said. "He never wanted to believe it. I admit that it sounds farfetched, but we *have* seen him."

"Believe what you want," he said in disbelief, shaking his head. "But I'm not waiting around to see who shows up here." He stepped around us and ran up the stairs, his feet forcefully hitting every step.

I buried my head in my hands. Moments later, Kevin was back down the stairs with his huge duffle bag slung over his shoulder. I stood when he stopped at the front door. "Where are you going?" I asked. "This is ridiculous, Kev."

He looked at me for a long moment, as his messy hair fell into his eyes. He still hadn't changed out of his uniform from the night before, and there was a speck of dried blood on the hem of his shirt. "Ridiculous, D? Me leaving instead of waiting for a convicted killer to show up at the door is ridiculous?" he asked, smiling without humor. "I'm being ridiculous because I'm more concerned that Matty is out of jail than you, and all you can think about is whether or not a ghost broke him out? I'm sorry, D. I can't do this. I can't believe that a ghost is beating you up, and I can't sit here and wait for Matty to come here to get us."

Lilly stared at me, waiting to see how I would respond, but I said nothing. He was deserting me. After all we had been through together the last four years, Kevin was leaving. I don't know what hurt more: the fact he was walking out, or him thinking that I was crazy. I turned and walked away from him, never looking back, when the door slammed firmly shut.

Becca Boucher

Chapter 24

Lilly

I stood at the bottom of the stairs, not knowing who to go after. The slam of the door was echoed by a bang in the kitchen and I turned to go after Daemon. He was standing at the sink, staring out across the backyard. I walked up behind him and wrapped my arms around his waist, and rested my forehead against his back. We stood like that in silence for what seemed like hours. I waited for his shoulders to stop shaking, and for the sound of his breathing to even out.

When he finally spoke, the words were hollow, resolute. "He walked out on us. What hurts more is that he thinks I'm crazy," Daemon said, shaking his head.

I reached up and softly put my hand on his cheek forcing him to turn and look me in the eye. "You're not crazy," I said, brushing a strand of hair from his eyes. "What we've seen takes years for people to come to terms with. If you're crazy, then I'm right there with you in line for the loony bin. I don't think it's coincidence that Matty escaped a day after you fought Aaron. I don't think any of this is coincidence at all."

I relaxed as his arms encircled me. He rested his chin on my head. The kitchen was bathed in sunlight, and the colors of fall leaves radiated in through the windows. Halloween was a week away, and it seemed like the icy rain of two days ago was a dream. I suddenly felt a chill on my arms. We needed to figure things out soon.

"Where do we go next?" Daemon asked, his voice close to my ear. "How do we figure out what he wants?"

I pulled back and looked him in the eyes. "We go see your mom."

Chapter 25

Daemon

I waited for Lilly to take a shower and get dressed. The whole time, things were running through my head: the fight with Aaron, Kevin leaving the way he did, and the news that Matty had escaped. None of it was making sense. I had no idea how my mother figured into all of this, but a confrontation with Kat or anyone else on the facility for that matter, was not in my best interest. In my present frame of mind I was liable to snap at any moment. It was only the calm blue eyes of Lilly that were keeping me sane. For once, she was the one in control. And I was unsure of how she was doing it. She came back into the kitchen as I was pouring our coffees, wearing the same clothes from the night before.

"Do you want to stop at your house and get some things?" I asked, setting a cup of coffee on the table in front of her.

She pulled out the kitchen chair and sat down. "We can after we go see your mom," she replied, lifting the cup to her lips.

I sat across from her and cradled my coffee cup between my hands, welcoming the warmth and the strong aroma. "Lil, in the spirit of honesty, I have no idea what seeing my mom is going to do for us. Her lucid moments are few and far between. You've seen it yourself. I don't know if it's background information that you're after or what, but I don't get how this is going to help," I said, suddenly feel anxious. "In the worst case scenario, it's just going to open us up to a confrontation with Kat. You just quit an hour ago, for heaven's sakes."

She reached across the table and took my hand. "The lady in white said that the veil is the weakest just before dawn, the place between awake and asleep. I was thinking that it could be weakest for your mom at any time. Her mind is so open that she can probably see ghosts at any time. Daemon … the picture of your aunt … it's the same lady I saw that night at my house. If we can get your mom talking, we might learn something."

I stared at Lilly's trusting eyes, felt the warmth of her hand in mine, and measured my words carefully, "Don't you think the key lies with Aaron? He's the one after us. If the lady in white is my aunt, how is she connected with this? The longer we sit here, the easier it is for Matty to find us." I pushed back from the table and walked over to the cabinet under the sink, taking out the bottle of Jack Daniel's. I set down my coffee mug to unscrew the cap just as Lilly knocked the bottle from my hand. "What the hell Lilly!" I turned to her and grabbed her arm at the same time. She looked down at my hand and pulled out of my grip.

"Daemon, stop with the booze and I'll stop the cutting," she said, her eyes boring into mine. She reached for the bottle, unscrewed the cap and poured the whole bottle of Jack down the sink. "Self destructive behavior is not going to help us," she continued, "We just have each other now." Tears were building up in the corners of her eyes, threatening to spill over. She had admitted her darkest secret to me.

I pulled her into my arms and buried my face in her hair. "I'll go get dressed."

She pulled back to look at me. "Is it a deal?"

I stared at the empty bottle lying in the sink, then reached out and pushed the sleeve of Lilly's sweater up, tracing the bandage with my free hand. Clearing my throat, I looked back to her eyes. "I'll try."

She looked at me with tired eyes. "That's all I ask, but try hard Daemon," she said, pulling her sleeve back down.

Forty five minutes later, we were walking down the hallway of the facility. Lilly's hand was so tight in mine that I had to fight the urge to let go of her. No one seemed to think anything about our appearance, but we had yet to see any sign of Kat. The closer we got to my mom's room the tension seemed to leave Lilly. As we reached the door, the sound of soft humming filtered out into the hallway. My mother was sitting in the chair by her bed, looking out over the treetops. She was humming a song and was badly out of tune. As we walked over the threshold, Lilly let go of my hand and softly pushed the door closed behind us. At the sound of the click, my mom looked up.

"Hi, kids," she said. "The trees are so beautiful this time of year, with all the golden hues and bright reds. Did you see the nurse with the med cart? I'm thirsty."

Lilly glanced at me with a sly smile. Mom was having a lucid day, but I wasn't sure if this was to our advantage or not. I crossed the room to her and placed my hand on her shoulder, then bent down to kiss her cheek. "Hi, Mom. We came to see you and check how you were doing."

"I know why you're here," she said, taking my hand. "I heard them talking in the hall. Matty's out. I don't know why everyone says it like it's a bad thing. School always gets out some time."

Lilly met my sideways glance. "Mrs. Kelly, have you heard from Matty?"

My mom shook her head from side to side. "No dear, why would I? And you can call me Mom, too. No use for formality at this time in my life."

Lilly crossed the room and sat on the edge of the bed closest to my mom, and I walked over to the window. The day was gorgeous, as all the trees glowed with the late October light. I turned back to look at my mom. She looked better than she had in weeks. Her hair was done up; it must have been her day for the hairdresser to come. She was wearing her best sweater and someone had taken the time to paint her fingernails. I leaned back on the window sill.

"Mrs. ... I mean ... Mom ... can you tell me more about Aunt Rita?" Lilly asked hopefully.

Mom looked at Lilly, and for a minute I thought our window had closed, but then she spoke, "Rita was a trip. She always said that she was more like a devil than a saint, but really, there wasn't a bad bone in her body. Did you know that her birthday was on Halloween, Daemon? She was my aunt, so that would make her Daemon's great aunt." She took a tissue out of her sleeve and used it to wipe the corner of her mouth. Then, she reached over and took Lilly's hand. "Daemon was named after Rita's husband, you know. Oh, my husband hated that, but my mother insisted. Did you know that they both had a fling with him?"

Lilly gave me an incredulous look. This was all news to me. "Mom, who had a fling with whom?"

But she ignored me, looking only at Lilly as she spoke. "Rita liked to read all about witches and what my grandfather called the Dark Arts. After high school, she ran off with her fling and joined a Wiccan religion. That was so unheard of in those days that everyone thought she was a communist. She ended up leaving him and then moved to Canada. My mother saw her once or twice after that and she sent home some letters."

Lilly was still holding my mom's hand staring intently at her as she spoke. I found myself wondering how much of this was real or a product of her senility. I pushed off from the window sill. "Mom, how come you never talked about Aunt Rita that much when I was growing up?"

She chuckled and shook her head as a cart clinked in the hall. "Is that the lunch cart? Lilly, be a dear and go see if it is."

Lilly glared at me. Yah, I got the message. "It's okay, Mom. They'll bring your lunch in." I sat on the bed next to Lilly, knowing that I had better not interrupt again. My mom glanced out the window and started ringing the tissue in her hands.

"Well, her father disowned her," Mom continued. "Not only had she run off with her sister's boyfriend, but she was also into that witch stuff. The family didn't understand it at all and any communication with her had to be in secret. The last thing my mother heard from her was that she had taken up with this Irish woman named Morgana. They were supposed to start their own group of believers. My mother went to her grave never hearing another thing from her. I used to see things as a girl. I called her the Women in White. I always thought it was Aunt Rita, but my mother would punish me for saying such things."

I noticed that Lilly's hand had slipped from my mother's. I looked at her face and it was ashen. Just then, there was a knock at the door. "Mrs. Kelly, I have your lunch tray." The aides' smile faded as she saw me. "Oh Daemon. I didn't know you were here. Would you like some lunch?"

I shook my head, "No we're fine." Lilly let go of my hand and walked over to the window. After I had my mom's lunch set up I walked over to her. "Are you okay?"

"Morgana," Lilly said, shaking her head from side to side. "That is too uncommon a name for it to be coincidence. The key to all this lies with Morgana."

I took her by her shoulders and looked directly into her eyes. "Lilly, your losing me here. Who is Morgana? I don't understand."

The look on her face was incredulous. "Remember the other day when we talked over breakfast and I told you about Aaron and how things had gotten weird?" she asked, then waited a moment for me to answer.

In that brief moment of silence, I remembered. "You said that he started to study Wicca and Celtic legends," I replied as a cold shudder swept through my body. "And he was fascinated by the Celtic Goddess Morgana."

She nodded her head as understanding dawned on my face. "Daemon, what if she is more than a "goddess"? What if she is a ghost herself? Communicating with other ghosts and even the living? What if she is controlling Aaron's soul somehow?"

I looked at our entwined fingers, trying to somehow form my next words so as not to alienate her. I really didn't think I was following her. I looked up into her red rimmed eyes. "Lilly … my mother … you know that she's not in her right mind. I don't think we can …"

"That's just it, Daemon," Lilly said, cutting me off. "She can in no way be making this up. She doesn't have the reasoning skills to. We hit her at a moment when her long term memory was strong and she was able to tell us about the past. How else could she have pulled that name out of her ass?" That was just it. Even I couldn't overlook the coincidence.

"Well, well, well, look what the cat dragged in," Kat said, intruding rudely, "if it isn't the King and Queen of inappropriate relationships."

Before I had a chance to respond to her, my mother was hurtling insults at Kat. "There's that filthy whore that chased down the train. Did you ever see a cat that looked more like a drag queen?" I glanced over at Lilly who had her hand over her mouth holding back a laugh. My mother's window of clarity was closed, but she still knew Kat was someone she didn't like.

"Mom … it's okay. Don't talk. I don't want you to choke," I said calmly.

She looked at me and huffed while Lilly went to guide her hand to the water glass. "Kat, if you have something to say I will gladly speak to you in the hall," Lilly said, looking in her direction.

Kat looked at me with hatred, then back at Lilly. "That won't be necessary," she replied sarcastically. "I just wanted to let you both know that we're aware of Matty's escape. There will be police patrolling the facility campus as well as our night crew." She look pointedly at Lilly as she spoke her next words. "I hope you don't regret your decision to resign, as well as your ill-timed hook up with this one. You're walking away from my friendship was the dumbest mistake that you ever made." She turned on her hells and walked toward the door. She hesitated and turned back around. "Don't you for a minute think that Aaron wouldn't want you to rot in hell for this, Lilly. You go ahead and keep fraternizing with the enemy. It just cements what I always told him about you."

Lilly crossed the room in three steps. Her face was suddenly inches from Kat's she spoke with venom that I hadn't thought could possibly come from her. "Go to hell, Kat! You can't judge a man by the sins of his brother! And you sure as hell can't speak for Aaron!" Kat raised her hand, reared back and let it fly at Lilly's face, but she grabbed her wrist just in time. "Don't you dare raise your hand to me! Get out of my face!" Lilly yelled, nose to nose with Kat. I grabbed Lilly's shoulders just as she pushed Kat out into the hallway.

Chapter 26

Lilly

The rest of the day passed in a blur. We spent it running around grabbing a few groceries for my house, and checking all the holistic and new age shops in Springfield. I wasn't sure what we were looking for, but I needed to find something that would explain the link between Morgana—whoever the hell she was—and Aaron. I ended up buying a book on Celtic lore and an encyclopedia of medicinal herbs, both on the advice of a hippie looking young women in a sweet smelling shop called Living Earth.

According to her, Morgana was the death goddess. She could cast a bewitching death spell on any man. It was also said that she is known to steal souls and transport them between the underworld and our realm.

Lovely. All this as well as the confrontation with Kat, ran through my mind as we made the hour and a half drive back to town. By the time we pulled into my driveway, it was dark. Neither Daemon nor I had spoken for the last thirty minutes. He wrapped his arm around my shoulders and I leaned into his embrace. His warmth, his soft breath on the nape of my neck, and his reassuring mummers all combined to relax my muscles and help me to draw a deep breath. "You okay?" he asked, concerned.

I turned to face him and softly pressed his lips to mine. "Much better now," I said, taking a long and deep breath. "Where do we go from here, Daemon? All we have to go on are fragmented stories, half-assed recollections, and a few encounters with Aaron's ghost. How can I make it stop?"

Becca Boucher

His finger lightly stroked the back of my hand. "We can't make it stop," he replied. "We can only try to solve the mystery, to figure out what he wants. But tonight, let me take care of you." He paused as he turned the key in the ignition and the car grew quiet. "Come on, I'll make us dinner."

I nodded as he let go of my hand and pushed open the driver's side door. I watched him as he made his way around the front of the car to meet me on my side, when suddenly he disappeared from my line of sight. At the same time, my door flew open almost soundlessly and I found myself thrown flat on the ground. I looked to my left and Daemon was lying on the ground in front of the car.

Directly in front of me was the most stunning woman that I had ever seen. Her flowing blonde hair was adorned with ivy vines and small red roses. She wore a white dress, embellished with gleaming embroidery of moons and stars. Her translucent skin seemed to radiate life, but her eye sockets were eerily vacant. To her right was Aaron, dressed in white with rays of light gleaming from his skin. His face betrayed no emotion.

When she spoke her voice was cold, but it maintained a musical quality. "Lilly, we finally meet face to face. Did you not know that you are supposed to bow before a high goddess?" Her long fingers dug into my scalp as she pressed my face closer to the ground.

I tried to speak, but couldn't find my voice and tears threatened to spill over from the corners of my eyes. *"Daemon!!!"* I managed to yell.

"Silly girl," the woman said, laughing without humor. "Your lover is fine … for now. Why do you not greet your husband? We have come so far to see you tonight."

I looked up as fear shook my body.

"My goddess," Aaron said, reaching for my hand. "You said that you would let me explain everything to her. We have frightened her once again."

She reached down and pulled me up by my chin to her eye level. I vaguely noticed that my feet had left the ground. Once again, my gaze returned to Daemon. "What have you done to him?" I asked, my voice weak with fear. "Who are you?"

She laughed as if I was of no consequence. "See, Aaron? You have waited too long. She knows nothing of her place in this plan … that her destiny is to get you to the other side of the moon … to your rightful place beside me." Her hands slid down my body, sizing me up, feeling my every curve, and her touch was like fire. "Your destiny, my child, is to be my conduit … to give your soul to free Aaron's. I am Morgana."

I gasped as she let go and I slid to the ground. She raised her left arm and threw a beam of light across the driveway. How could the neighbors not see this? Daemon started to push himself up off the ground, but then Morgana directed the beams toward him, sweeping him to the side of the porch and back into unconsciousness.

I lunged forward, as a stifling sob escaped from my lips. Morgana walked toward the tunnel of light. "Aaron, see how she cries out for him? Has she ever grieved for you in such a way?"

"You bitch!" I shouted at her as she walked farther into the light. "I cried every day for him! For over a year, I was lost in my own grief. Now, it's my turn to cry for the living."

Suddenly, Aaron's unusually cold, clammy grip was on my arm and turned me around to face him. "You must not speak to the goddess in such tones," he said as his eyes glowed.

When I looked back over my shoulder, she was gone as the effervescent light sparkled into nothingness. All that was left was the void that was Aaron's eyes. Why had I not noticed it before? In life, his eyes had been an engaging blue, but in death they were dark black, staring into my soul. He pulled me to his rock hard chest, holding me against his cold body, almost burning my skin where it touched his.

"Morgana was right," Aaron said, trying to explain. "The fall equinox is the feast of all saints ... we need to pass through on that day. I need you to free me ... to guide me."

"Aaron, you never believed there was anything after life before," I said, looking into the dark void of his eyes. "What's out there? What lies on the other side of the moon?"

"Silly girl," Aaron said, laughing without humor. "I never believed in the traditional way that you did. Shortly before my death, I met Morgana in her human form. She explained to me that the souls of men give her power, and I could share in that power. It was only coincidence that Matthew freed me that night. Morgana lined up the cards and fate."

"She lined up the cards?" I asked as my mind whirled. "I don't understand, Aaron. How am I connected to this?" He let go of my arm and ran his ice-cold hand down my face. My skin felt frostbit at his touch.

"The alter of the damned, Quaker Cemetery, the one with the spiders carved in the gates," he said in a monotone voice. "The seven pillars, the seventh gate of hell. We need to finish this there at midnight on All Hollows Eve." He stopped speaking for a minute and rubbed the back of his neck. "I never counted on him figuring into this picture." He gestured with a nod of his head toward Daemon, who was lying still on the ground.

Suddenly, one thing that he said stood out in my mind ... the seventh gate of hell. "Aaron, it's not the other side of the moon. It's not the throne of Heaven that she is promising, it's Hell. You will be damned." Then, beyond all reason, I added, "And there is no way that the Devil will give you his throne."

Abruptly, he grabbed me by the back of my neck. "Lilly, the throne ... her throne ... will be ours." Daemon stirred on the ground behind Aaron and rose to his feet, then lunged for Aaron. He pulled him off me and spun him around. Aaron reacted by pushing Daemon up against the side of the house. "And you! Are you enjoy my wife? What she needs to do must be done alone." Still holding Daemon to the wall, he looked over his shoulder at me. "You *will* be at the altar on All Hallows Eve ... alone. I will make sure of that. Morgana freed our insurance policy and he will bring you."

"It was you. You broke my brother out of jail," Daemon said through clenched teeth. Abruptly, a cold flash of light and wind blew up the driveway, bringing back the tunnel of light Morgana had walked into ... and Aaron was gone.

The next thing I knew, I was shaking in Daemon's arms. Somehow, we had found our way into the house and were sitting on my couch. Daemon's shirt front was drenched from my tears, and his beautiful dark hair was messed up from his habit of running his hand through it when he was nervous. Ghosts seemed to be the norm for us, but this time it was the ultimatum ... and the chilling appearance of Morgana ... that had me suffering a panic attack. Daemon's chin rested on my head. The steady beating of his heart and the calming whispers of his breath were starting to ground me.

"Lil, it's okay, baby," Daemon said, tightening his arms around me. "I'm not leaving you to fight this alone."

"Do we have to fight this? Can't we ignore it and hope for them to go away?" I asked, raising my head to look into his eyes, memorizing every gorgeous feature of his face.

"Lil, I'll be the first to admit that I want nothing more than for them to go away," he said, taking my hand into his. "Up until a few weeks ago, I never even believed in ghosts ... but I didn't believe in love, either." He leaned in and kissed me softly on the corner of my lips. "But my gut tells me that there is no way in hell, literally, that they are going away. And who can we go to? We can't walk into a police station and say that we're being chased and blackmailed by ghosts, can we? They would lock us both up for sure."

I chuckled, snuggled onto his chest. "What can we do then, Daemon?"

He brushed the hair back away from my face and kissed my cheek, trailing small kisses down to the nape of my neck.

Becca Boucher

"We have a week to figure that out. Right now, we make dinner before we starve to death. Then, we go to bed and make love until we fall asleep, because if we *are* being haunted by delusional, homicidal ghosts, I want to make sure that I spend what time I have left on this earth with the love of my life." With that he pushed me back into the couch and cupped both my cheeks gently into his hands. His lips met mine and before I had time to think, we were kissing more passionately than ever before. My hands tangled in his hair, as my tears fell on his cheeks. Nothing mattered at that moment: the threat of Aaron, the fear of being judged by Kat, not even the reality of Matty having broken out of jail mattered. All that registered in my mind in that moment was the feel of his lips on my breasts … and the soft reassuring mummer of his voice declaring of his love.

***

I woke up some time in the early morning hours, and the sky was still dark and Daemon's arms were wrapped around me. The stillness was almost palpable. The memory of last night was still fresh in my mind. I threaded my fingers through Daemon's hair, then leaned over and pressed his lips to mine. He stirred in his sleep, turned over, and releasing me from his arms. I lay next to him, taking in his woodsy cologne, nestling close to his back, when the early morning light started to tinge the sky.

I rose from the bed, made my way into the bathroom, and looked into the mirror. The women who looked back at me was thinner, had a few more worry lines, but also bore the glow of a night of love making. I brushed my hair and pulled it back into a tight pony tail. When I splashed water on my face, I noticed the razor blade on the back of the sink. Picking it up, I forced myself to think of how many times I turned to it, piercing my skin to let out the pain. Then, my eyes moved to the scar on my left arm. It had healed well in the last week. I looked back up into the mirror, trying to see what Daemon saw in my green eyes and pale, rose-tinted skin. I smiled at how plump my lips were from all his kisses. Kisses that did more to kill the pain than this razor had ever done. Slowly, I released it, letting it fall into the trash can and pushed it down below the rest of the trash, pushing all my insecurities down along with it.

I opened the medicine cabinet and took out the last three bottles that had belonged to Aaron. Slowly, I set two of them on the growing pile in the trash can. The third, a bottle of his favorite aftershave, I poured down the sink, watching the liquid make a slow decent down the drain. Crossing to the window, I opened it and pushed up the screen. I pulled my arm back and chucked the empty aftershave bottle across the yard. I giggled as it made contact with the garage and shattered, purging myself of the last reminders of Aaron, and clearing the way for the love that I so desperately wanted.

Becca Boucher

Chapter 27

Daemon

I woke up to an empty bed empty, as the smell of coffee made its way up the stairs and filled the room. Last night had been a mixture of emotions, ranging from fear, to anger, and love. We had spent the better half of the early morning hours making love and talking. Lilly's scent still lingered on my skin.

I pushed up from the bed and grabbed my jeans from the floor, and pulled them on as I made my way into the hallway. In the past, I had nothing waiting for me besides Kevin and a bottle of Jack. Now, I couldn't wait to head downstairs to find my Lilly. Being in her house felt right, and no ghost could make me believe otherwise.

In the kitchen, I found her sitting at the table with a big cup of coffee and the books that we had purchased yesterday. She looked up when I walked into the room, her eyes glowing. "You want some coffee?" she asked.

"Looks like you have been busy," I said, nodding at the stack of books setting on the table as I sat down. "Did you find anything good?"

She rose and smiled at me over her shoulder as she made my coffee. "A little bit. Morgana can be traced back to both the Celtic and Welsh legends, and we know that Aaron was interested in these things shortly before his death." She sat back down at the table and pushed my coffee toward me. "Here is where it gets scary. This book traces Morgana back to Morgan LeFay, the same Morgan LeFay from King Author's day, which I admit might be a stretch. But then it goes on to say that she can cast a destroying curse on any man and is a conduit between this world and the next."

I reached across and took her hand in mine and watched her intently as she spoke, mesmerized by her green eyes.

"But I was thinking, what does this have to do with All Saints Day, Halloween, and the moon? What's the connection?" She stopped and flipped to a marked page in the book. "Then, I found this. Moon worship predated sun worship in almost every clan society; all of the ancients had moon goddesses. Egypt had Isis or Seshat; the Eskimos called her Sedna; the Chinese called her Shing Moon; and the Celts called her Morgana. Rituals were always held in her honor and usually at the same time as the summer solstice, the Spring Equinox, Fall Equinox and Samhain ... or Halloweeen." She turned the book toward me so that I could see the paragraphs and pictures that she was referring to. There was no doubt that all these dates were known for their full moons.

"Then, my mind drifted back to the first time that I had met Aaron. The moon had certainly been bright, but last night there had been cloud cover. Also, two other things were bothering me ..."

"Lilly, why would she choose Aaron?" I interrupted. "Can you think of any reason that he would be linked to an ancient moon goddess? Why had he started this fascination with the moon and Celtic rites, anyway? And why are you some kind of key?"

She drank the last of her coffee and stared out the window. Her green eyes were somber and troubled. I rose from the table and crossed the room to her, then pulled her into my arms. She sighed heavily and nestled herself into my bare chest before she spoke. "I don't know, but I need to ask him."

I stepped back and held her at arm's length. "Ask him?" I asked, incredulous. "How do you plan to ask him? He's always showed up on his terms." Something that looked like fear suddenly registered in her eyes. I wasn't sure if it was from my reaction, or the possibility of having to initiate contact with Aaron.

"Daemon, are you mad at me?" she asked, raising an eyebrow.

"God no, Lilly," I replied, pulling her back in my arms, then kissed the top of her head. "Why would you think that?" The ticking of the clock on the wall seemed to echo through the room. It was that silent. When she answered, her voice was merely a whisper. "I don't want you to be jealous when I talk to him. I don't want you to be worried."

I had to hold in the chuckle that rose in the back of my throat. "Lilly, trust me. I'm not jealous of Aaron ... or his ghost. I know you don't have feelings for him anymore." Or did she? The thought crept unwelcomed into my mind.

"Oh, thank God, Daemon," she replied, breathing a sigh of relief. "After all this I can't lose you now. I just ... it has to be done. Like the vision I had the night you followed me home. I saw the events that led to his killing. If he can show me that, maybe there is a way to ask him why. Why the deceit? Why the fascination with an edgy religion when he never believed in mainstream religion while he was alive? And I think I know how we can get him to come."

She leaned into me and kissed me passionately her hands cupping my ass. I backed her up against the kitchen sink and pulled her shirt up over her head, longing to feel every inch of her body against mine. We slid to the floor, a tangled mess of clothes and limbs. She moaned softly as I bit her ear and rolled on top of her.

"Are you going to let me in on your idea?" I asked, nibbling on her ear.

She giggled as she parted her legs for me to join with her. "This is a clue," she replied, giggling.

A little confused and intrigued at the same time, I slid into her. "Hmmm, Miss Lawson, are you using me?"

She giggled. "Never, Mr. Kelly. I'm just falling in love with you," she said, and from the look in her eyes—filled with so much intensity—I knew it was true as we spent the rest of the morning making love.

A time later I lay across Lilly's bed, waiting for her to finish her shower. I was flipping through the book that she had been looking at earlier, wondering just what she had up her sleeve. She never did get around to telling me; we were too preoccupied.

My thoughts were interrupted by the ringing of my cell phone. "Hello," I asked, listening. Silence. "Hello?"

"D? Where are you man?" I sat up at the sound of Kevin's voice just as Lilly walked in from the bathroom drying her hair. "I'm at Lilly's. What's up, man? You okay?" I asked, concerned. I sat up on the bed, listening intently for his answer. Lilly sat on the edge of the bed, listening.

His voice cracked when he answered. "Oh, thank God. I came back ... to apologize to you, and ... oh, shit man! You have to get over to your house ... now!"

I stood up, grabbed my wallet and keys and shoved them into my pockets. From the sound of his voice, it wasn't good. "Okay, man," I said, slipping into my shoes. "We'll be right there. And Kev, it's okay, man. I understand, things have been going crazy fast and ... well ... thank you for coming back."

Lilly looked at me with concern in her eyes. On the other end of the call, Kevin mumbled something unintelligible and hung up.

"What's wrong, Daemon?" Lilly asked, concerned.

I shook my head. "I don't know. That was Kevin, he just said to get over to my house ASAP. He sounded shocked. You almost done?"

She started pulling her hair back into a pony tail. "Yah, just let me get my purse."

On the twenty minute drive over to my house, Lilly outlined her plan to get Aaron to visit us before next week. What she said made sense when I thought about it. The other times that Aaron had showed up, Lilly and I were always together. With the exception of last night and the first time he paid me a visit, we were getting romantic. But he only appeared in each new place once: in the car, the parking lot at the facility, and in the house. The other times that Lilly had seen him, she was alone and just waking up. So, we had to find a place that was important to him, and where we hadn't been together. The logical answer was the Camaro.

On the night that he had showed her the events of his murder, she had been in the Camaro. He had spent years restoring the thing. She also thought that we needed a night when the moon was full. It couldn't hurt, anyway. We were just trying to figure out the best course of action to take when I pulled the truck around the corner of my street. As soon as I saw my house, the reason for Kevin's distress was evident. State police cruisers littered my driveway. Caution tape wrapped its way around the front porch, and members of the local fire department were hosing down the charred remains of my shed.

I jerked the truck to a stop, jumped out and grabbed Lilly's hand. Even before we made it across the yard, Kevin grabbed us both into a huge bear hug. He was closely followed by a police officer wearing plain clothes. "Daemon, I thought you guys were in the house," Kevin said, panicked. "I got here just when the shed exploded and the front porch was already engulfed in flames. I just ..." He stopped as his voice started to shake, so Lilly took his hand.

"Mr. Kelly?" a voice asked behind me. I turned and it was the officer.

"Yes?" I asked, shocked, but trying to stay calm.

"I'm officer Black with the State Fire Marshal's office. You were not home at the time of the fire, correct?"

I stared at him with an incredulous look.

"Well, I think that fact is evident," Lilly said, sensing my agitation. "We stayed at my house last night, Officer Black." She glanced at me sideways. "Do you have any idea how this started?"

He took out a small notebook. "At this time, no. But due to the relationship between Mr. Kelly and a certain escaped convict, we have an idea. And who may you be?"

"Lilly Lawson, Mr. Kelly's girlfriend," she said, holding out her hand for him to shake.

The officer looked up from his notebook and cleared his throat. "Ms. Lawson, are you ..."

"Yes, I am aware of the relationship between Daemon and the convict," she said, then continued, "and, yes. I am *that* Lilly Lawson. Therefore, I also have a connection to Matthew Spencer."

He stared at the three of us for what seemed like an eternity, then said, "Well I think the situation is pretty self explanatory, then," he said, turning toward the house. "The damage is confined to the outside structure and to the front porch, but I would advise that you stay elsewhere tonight because of the smoke and water damage ... and because Mr. Spencer is still on the run."

"I think I have that covered, sir," I said, rolling my eyes.

He cleared his throat once again. "Well, if you feel like you are in need of police protection for the next forty eight hours, that can be arranged. We are hoping that the suspect will be caught quickly."

"That will not be necessary, Officer Black," Lilly said. "Mr. Spencer has no clue as to the relationship of his brother and I. Therefore, he would have no reason to come looking for Daemon at my house. I think we'll be fine."

Officer Black took a card from his pocket and handed it to me. "If you change your mind, you can reach me at my office at this number," he replied, then turned and walked away to speak to one of the fire fighters.

I ran my hand through my hair and said, "Lilly, if he got out the way we think he got out, then he most certainly knows about our relationship."

She looked at me, surprised. "Daemon, do you think that the police can stop him? After everything we figured out this morning, their interference would be useless. We need to start to get answers and we can't do that with armed babysitters."

I looked at her and then at Kevin, who was more confused than ever. "You're right, Lil," Kevin said, stepping between us. "I take it that you two still think ghosts broke out Matty? Guys, bear with me. I need to take this slow."

I slapped him on the shoulder and smiled. "Kev, brace yourself because we have a lot to fill you in on."

An hour later, we were sitting in a back booth at Applebees explaining everything that we knew to Kevin. Lilly and I sat across from him and watched as his facial expressions turned from doubt, to fear and, finally, to understanding. "So, you don't know why Lilly is the key to this?" he asked, trying to understand.

"Nope. It's still a huge mystery," I said, shaking my head. "But with a little luck, we'll know more soon. I don't expect you to be in on this, Kev."

"I have a feeling the more human interference that we bring, the harder it will get to lure Aaron out," Lilly chimed in. "I thought it would be best for me to go it alone, but Daemon won't have it." Just then, I reached over and put my hand on her leg.

"Well, if you say so," he said with a chuckle, watching us. "It's not like I was biting at the bit to be included in this insanity. So, you have a week until Halloween. That's just one week to figure out why he needs Lilly there and why this all came about in the first place." Kevin laughed without humor, then added, "I don't envy your situation, guys." He picked up his beer and drained the last of it and motioned to the waitress to bring him another. Then, he looked at my soda. "No Jack in that coke, bro?"

I looked at Lilly, and said, "We have a deal." Her smile warmed me to the core. "No self destructive behaviors."

Kevin laughed again as the waitress set his beer down on the table. "So, conjuring up ghosts and willingly meeting them in deserted cemeteries doesn't count as self destructive behavior?" I kicked him under the table. Kevin jumped, almost spilling his beer. "What the hell! What did you do that for, D?"

Lilly jumped in to calm the moment. "What Daemon is trying to say, is that we both have addictions that we need to cure … whether or not Aaron and Morgana can be described as self destructive behavior is up for debate. We didn't go looking for them, remember?"

He shook his head. "I guess so. Okay … look … I'm not volunteering for any ghostly mission or night time romps. Hell, I don't even know if I believe this yet, but if you guys need me, I'm here. No questions asked, bro. My paramedic skills will be at your disposal." He made an over-the-top flourish and bow.

"Thanks, Kev," I said, smiling. "I really appreciate all of this … and don't worry about Matty. I don't think you're even on his radar."

"Thanks D," he grimaced. "I forgot about that."

The ride to Lilly's was quiet. We dropped Kevin off at his sister's house and I pointed my truck the direction of home … Lilly's house. After I retrieved some personal belongings from my house, the fire department wouldn't let me in. We didn't even have to talk about it; we both knew where I belonged.

Shortly before we reached her street, I pulled off into an open field known as the flats. The view was unobstructed and the three-quarter moon was gorgeous. After the unsettling weather last week, now there was not a cloud in the sky. The stars were bright and seemed close enough to touch. Lilly looked over at me. "Why are we stopping?"

I took her hand. "Can we walk for a while? Out in the field? The night is so nice," I asked.

She smiled, giving me a slight nod and we slowly got out of the truck.

We walked into the middle of the field hand in hand. The night was cool and smelled like fall. Halfway out, I stopped and pulled her into my side, closed my eyes and buried my face in her hair. "The calm before the storm," I whispered.

"You really believe that, don't you, Daemon?" she asked, looking into my eyes.

I sighed heavily. "If we thought things were tough before, I have the feeling that it's just going to get tougher from here on out." I placed a finger under her chin and tilted her face up toward mine, then continued, "Lilly, I just want you to know that my intentions were nothing but pure when I followed you home on the day of the sentencing. You had just looked so ... so lost in the courtroom. I wanted you to know that I was nothing like him. I only realized on that day that we worked at the same place. I never had anything planned and I wasn't stalking you," I stammered.

"Shush," she said.

"Let me finish," I said, placing a finger gently on her lips. "I fell in love with you because of who you are ... the beautiful person you are inside and out. No matter how this ends or who says what, never think otherwise. In the three short weeks since you've become my world, Lilly Lawson, I finally learned how to live."

A single tear rolled down her cheek as the moonlight played with the golden highlights in her hair, making us glow in its light. "I know, Daemon," she said in a husky voice. "A part of me always knew that, or I never would have pulled my car over." She took both of my hands into hers, then kissed our entwined fingers. "I believe in fate, Daemon, even more than I believe in God. I love you, Daemon Kelly."

We kissed in the middle of the field for what seemed like hours ... sweet, honest kisses. Then, I swept her up in my arms and carried her back to the truck. Whatever next week had in store for us, we had this moment ... the calm before the storm.

Chapter 28

Lilly

The dreams had stopped after I started sleeping with Daemon. It had been a relief not to wake in fear and reach for the razorblade, but that also meant that we were in the dark as to what Aaron's next moves were. He always seemed to speak to me in those dreams. We were three short days before All Hallows Eve and, still he hadn't appeared.

Daemon and I had tried sitting in the Camaro, taking it out on back roads at night and pushing the limits of the engine. I held Daemon's hand as he drove, certain that the sacrilege of such an act would bring Aaron to us, but it never did. I researched the Quaker cemetery and found that it had been used in the past for rituals and rites by all sorts of cult, fringe groups, as well as being a favorite party area for local teens. Also, there were at least two newspaper articles linking it to murders.

These were all comforting thoughts, for sure, but even more disconcerting were the things we dug up on *Samhain* or Halloween. The Eve of Samhain was the Celtic New Year. There were also links between Druid and Celtic celebrations of the feast and human sacrifice. Daemon's hand clenched mine as we read about bonfires and the otherworld. To some, Samhain Eve was a night of dread and danger, but to others it was the holiest of times. The dead returned, both good ghosts and demons walked the earth, and the future could be seen. At this juncture of the old year and the new, our world and the otherworld opened up to each other. The dead returned, ghosts and demons walked the Earth and the future could be seen.

Also disconcerting was that they needed a living link for wandering souls to pass through, as these souls were unable to pass through on their own. My roll was suddenly becoming clear, and Daemon pledged he wouldn't let me go alone.

As the days flew by and the hours ticked down, we explored each other more and more. We talked into the wee hours of the morning, sat by his mother's bed for countless hours, and caught up on things couples would take months of dating to do. No topic was taboo or too hard to discuss, It was if we had no time for the trivial.

We took in every story his mother told us, whether it was rational or not. She told us a little more about Aunt Rita and how spiritual she was. I still held on to the hope that she could tell us one little thing that would help us to make sense of it all.

On the night before the final day, October 30, we went to bed early. The moon was a sliver away from full. As I lay in Daemon's arms and his fingers ran through my hair, I spoke in the darkness. "Aaron, I really need to speak with you. Please, I beg you to visit me ... to visit us."

Daemon wiped away my tears with the back of his hand. "It's okay, Lilly," he said tenderly.

"No, it's not, Daemon," I said with a sigh. "What if I decided not to show up? What if this was all in our delusional minds? Will Matty really come here to drag me there?"

He rolled over to face me and said, "I won't leave you, no matter how this turns out. They're real and this is all a part of their game ... and if we don't face it head on, we'll never free ourselves."

I had nothing left to say, so I buried my head in his neck and closed my eyes.

I woke as I was being yanked from the bed. The room slowly came into focus around me and I struggled to find if it was real or just a dream. When I looked up, Aaron was standing in front of me, tangible and cold. "Aaron," I whispered.

He reached out and slid his cold fingers down my cheek. "Lilly. The time is near," he said, his voice breaking the stillness of the night. "Are you going to come willingly tomorrow night?"

"Yes," I said, my voice barely audible, "but tell me why. Why do you need me? Why did you turn to the darkness that I see in your eyes?"

He led me over to the window and opened it, letting the cold mist fill the room. He pointed toward the moon and looked back to where Daemon lay sleeping on the bed. "Not here," he said, his voice as quiet as the edge of a knife. He took my hand and plunged us both from the window. My scream was cut off by a gust of wind that pulled me higher into the sky, flying over the treetops. Moments later, we settled on the grass close to the train tracks, like the first night I found myself with his ghost.

He traced the faint scar from my last cut and asked, "Do you ever wonder if you will still bleed? I don't bleed anymore Lilly. I feel no pain."

My legs betrayed me and I sat on the ground. Cold in just Daemon's old T-shirt.

"Do you love him Lilly?" he asked as I looked into his vacant eyes.

"Yes. I love him," I replied, taking a deep breath, letting the cool air fill my lungs. "I don't want him to lose me."

"Kat was right on some things," he said, looking away, "but she never would have been the one."

I brushed a tear from my eye. "Why, Aaron ? Why Morgana? Did she appear to you when you were alive?"

He looked up at the moon as he spoke, detached from all emotion. "She came to me six months before my death. In her human form, she was radiant, breathtaking. I thought that I had seduced her, but it was the other way around. She taught me about the connection of the moon and the divine power of her godhood. When she revealed her true self to me, I just knew." I felt myself grow sick as I listened to him talk. "When she told me about Scotland, I knew that I had to go. We hatched up a plan and sold it to my boss. I picked that fight with you so that I could get you out of the way. My true time of death was supposed to be in her ancestral home, but that bastard messed things up by killing me here." He turned to me then, and his eyes glowed with a sinister light. "You know why she chose me, Lilly? Because I didn't believe anything. Your God is weak. When we take the throne, the world will see our true power."

I stared at him, unable to believe what I was hearing. "But she's evil, Aaron. Can't you see that? She has your killer working with you now. It's a game of domination. Leave me alone and leave her alone, too. Find your own way to the other side of the moon."

He picked me up by my upper arms to look me in the eye. "And you sleep with his brother!" he accused. "In order to finally free myself from this world, we need his blood … and we need your release. You need to release my soul by forfeiting your own."

I stared at him, shaking in his grip. My voice was a fragment of what it could be. "You will kill me? I never betrayed you in life. I don't understand, Aaron." Tears cascaded down my cheeks as pain filled my body. I saw a chink in his armor, a true glimmer of pain in his eyes. He lifted me farther from the ground and threw me as if I were a ragdoll.

The next thing I knew, I was standing back in my bedroom looking out over the backyard, but his words resounded from the darkness in reply, "I don't understand, either."

I threw myself on the bed and my sobs woke Daemon. "He finally came?" he asked.

I nodded in response.

"I love you," Daemon replied. As the dim light of dawn trickled into the room, October 31 had arrived.

Chapter 29

Dameon

The hike took just under twenty minutes. We found it on the map, surprisingly, since the road it intersected didn't exist. It seemed surreal to come upon this cemetery in the clearing of the woods. It was forgotten by time, but remarkably well kept.

Lilly kept checking the folded paper that she held tightly in her hands. She almost laughed as she turned to look at me. "I thought this place was supposed to be scary," she said, shaking her head. "With all of the stories from the kids who partied here and all the murders, you would think that it would be horrifying, but it's just a normal cemetery."

I held tightly to the waist band of her jeans and pulled her into my arms. "Normal?" I asked, unable to believe her nonchalance. "We were told to come here by a ghost and a crazy goddess, and there's nothing normal about a cemetery deep in the woods." I looked up as the sky started to fade into the early evening twilight. The dense tree cover made it darker than it should be, and the wind was picking up.

Lilly looked at me with uncertainty in her eyes and said, "I think I'm meant to go in alone." She rung the paper tighter in her hands. "I'm scared, Daemon." And truth be told, I was too. "Don't let me die, Daemon."

I pulled the gun from my backpack and loaded it. I wasn't sure if guns were any good against ghosts, but I felt better holding it. Kissing the top of Lilly's head, taking in her sweet scent, I made a promise that I hoped I could keep, "I will never let anyone or anything hurt you, Lilly. I promise."

Becca Boucher

I watched her as she made her way into the clearing and slowed, almost as if she had forgotten what we were doing here. The cemetery was bordered on three sides by the woods and edged by ancient stone walls. The headstones ringed the outer perimeter, leaving the middle an open clearing. In an area of seven trees in the middle was a raised knoll. It formed a sort of altar that had pillars at the four corners. The pillars were stout with ruins carved into the sides.

Lilly looked up at the pink and purple sunset and stopped. It was a funny time to be having a moment. I was mystified as she bent down and ran her hands through the wet grass and pressed them to her face, oblivious to my presence on the other side of the clearing. I was supposed to be back by the entrance, but I was afraid to leave her alone. Then, she knelt and crossed herself. I didn't know if it would help, but it certainly couldn't hurt. In the last week she spent a lot of the time alone praying for strength ... or a miracle, but I know that miracles are hard to come by. I got mine when I met her. I would have prayed with her but, like this meeting, it was something that she felt she was supposed to do alone. I watched, but what she did next surprised me ... and I don't surprise easily.

She stood up and stepped farther into the clearing and seemed to look straight at me and through me at the same time. "Aaron, here I am!" she yelled, trying to get his attention instead of waiting for the moon. "I'm tired of this! If you want me so badly, then come and get me! I know you can hear me!" Then, her voice was merely a whisper, "You won, you bastard."

I lowered my gun and stepped out of the brush, into her line of sight. That's when Matthew stepped from the shadows and shot me. The shot startled her and the pain blinded me. I fell to the ground as she ran to my side. It was a clean shot right through my shoulder. They both reached me at the same time. Lilly clung to my side and her tears mixed with my blood, just as my brother ran up.

"The goddess told you to come alone, didn't she?" Matthew's deep voice bellowed through the clearing as he pulled Lilly up by her arm.

Lilly's eyes met mine, as tears streamed down her face. "Let me go!" she yelled. "It was never said either way! I need to help him!"

Suddenly, Matty threw back his head and laughed. "There's no hope for him … or you." His eyes were vacant, as if he was in a trance.

I tried to speak, but my head spun with pain. "Matty, you won't make it out of this alive, either."

He glanced my way. "Jail or death? Which one would you choose, brother?" he said, pointing the barrel of the gun directly at me.

I stared deeply into his eyes and replied, "It looks like that choice is being made for me."

Lilly's cries grew more urgent as she struggled to break free of his grasp. I vaguely noticed the sky growing darker as another voice spoke from the distance, "Enough."

Matty froze, releasing Lilly's hand and dropped to the ground in a prone position.

Lilly dropped to my side, and pressed her hand against my shoulder, crying softly as she tried to stop the blood.

I looked up and in the middle of the knoll stood Morgana, clothed in white, but she wasn't alone. Behind her to her left was Aaron, his clothes looked old, blood stained and torn. Farther to the back of the knoll against the stone fence were faint figures, wisps of light floating toward Morgana, taking form as they drew near.

I pushed up on my elbows to see better, not sure if I was hallucinating from blood loss or if we were being surrounded by an army of ghosts. Lilly trembled next to me, as tears fell silently upon her cheeks.

"Rise, my servant," Morgana said. Her voice echoed off the trees as Matty rose from the ground. He walked in mechanical steps toward the knoll as Morana spread her arms wide. He stopped in front of her and she took a golden dagger from her pocket and struck him on the head with the hilt. He fell to the ground as Lilly stifled a scream with a hand over her mouth.

As the forms came closer, we could see that they were people in various styles of dress from different ages. The closer that they came to Morgana, the more humanoid they appeared as they lined the outside edges of the knoll, forming a tight square.

"Lilly. I am glad that you decided to come and join us tonight. I guess your connection to Aaron was strong," Morgana said, opening her arms wide. "Rise and come to me, my child."

Lilly shook her head in silent protest, holding tightly to my side.

Morgana laughed, and her congregation parted, forming a path. "You don't have a choice, dear." She was in front of us in no time. From her outstretched arms, a beam of light emitted from her fingertips. Suddenly, the light encased Lilly and I, raised us from the ground and brought us to the center of the knoll. The circle closed tightly around the perimeter again, and the faces were clearer to us now. Lilly spoke for the first time since Morgana had appeared. "Fairies? Are you a fairy queen?" she asked Morgana.

Morgana nodded her head with no trace of humor and said, "Faye, fairy, ghost … call us what you like. We are the conduit to the other world. In fact, we live among you. My more pleasant counterpart visited you once, and I think she told you that at some points, the veil is weaker and that we can be seen." She walked away from us and pushed Matty over with the toe of her shoe.

My bleeding had stopped and for the time being, I felt as if my head was beginning to clear.

"Sometimes," Morgana continued, "it is even possible to stumble into our world. Aaron had done just that and I took a liking to him." She stopped next to Aaron and kissed his lips.

"I suppose that I was drawn to his brilliance and his disbelief in anything other than the scientific; I found it fascinating.

"Soon, I taught him about my kind and how he could have true immortality, but he wanted you, too." Morgana turned to face Lilly with contempt. "And you, Lilly, believed in the Christian God. I could not convince him that you would hold him back." The circle of her believers nodded their heads in agreement. "Then came this one," she said, stopping to look down at Matty. Life was slowly fading from him as he lay at her feet. "He stole Aaron from me. Dying at another's hand made Aaron's passage to me impossible. He needs a clear pass." The congregation nodded their agreement, closing in tighter to the knoll. "So, tonight he pays for his sin ... and you, Lilly, will release Aaron once and for all."

Lilly looked up at her for the first time. "How?" she asked. Her voice quivered as she asked the question we had both been asking all week.

"By making a choice," Morgana said, looking at us with hard, cold eyes. "It always comes down to a choice, Lilly." She walked over to Matty and lifted his arm. Then, she lifted the knife and ran the blade across his veins, releasing a torrent of his blood into a silver chalise. She turned toward Aaron, "Come. Stand beside me, love."

Even though I had suffered at the hands of my brother over the years, tears run down my cheeks as my brother's life left his body. Lilly and I rose from the ground hand in hand. Lilly prayed for Matty softly under her breath, asking God for his forgiveness and for the angels to take him. After the chalice was filled, Aaron held it up to the light of the moon and Morgana chanted in Gaelic. The figures around the edges of the knoll knelt together as Morgana turned to us.

"Now, Lilly, it's your choice," she said. "Free Aaron from this world by mixing your blood, your soul, with the blood of his killer, allowing Daemon to walk away from here and life to return to Aaron. Then, Aaron will meet his destiny at my hands." She lovingly glanced at Aaron, and the congregation nodded their heads in agreement.

"And if I choose otherwise?" Lilly asked, bravely squaring her shoulders and looking Morgana directly in the eye.

Morgana laughed. "You won't."

Lilly looked at me and unclenched her hand. In it was a necklace that I remembered instantly. It was my mother's, the virgin and child surrounded by a Celtic love knot. Her eyes bore deeply into mine, begging for understanding, but I was lost. She left my side and walked up to face Morgana. She stopped three short steps from her and slipped the necklace over her head. Suddenly, the clouds covered the sky as the wind picked up and torrents of rain fell upon us all. The moon was no longer visible and the congregation of faye around the knoll started to fade.

Morgana looked at Lilly with hatred. "You have chosen wrong, Lilly," she said, raising the dagger. Suddenly, the chalice slipped from Aaron's hands and Matty's blood spilled upon the ground.

"Stop!" Aaron yelled abruptly, but something else caught my eye. Over the east wall, an army of angels flew in, shining in all of their glory as their magnificent wings spread to the sky. In their midst was Rita, her own wings glowing golden against the rain darkened sky.

That's when all hell broke loose. Aaron pushed Lilly to the ground and she crawled on all fours to me. I grabbed her and held on to her for dear life as flashes of light shot across the sky and torrents of rain began to fall. The majority of the Fae ran to the front of the knoll and made a wall around Morgana as their small hands clenched into fists and claws. Aaron picked up the golden dagger from the ground and crouched in front of his queen. Morgana. A small group of Fae backed off and joined Rita. Instead of claws, they seemed to grow small incandescent wings as they hovered in front of the congregation of angels.

Morgana lifted her arms and commanded her army to fight. They charged the angels as one, emitting light from their eyes as their razor sharp claws sliced at anything in their path. The angels advanced, quiet and commanding, walking straight ahead, reflecting the blinding light with their wings. One of them fell and her beautiful wings were shredded by the angry claws of a particularly nasty looking Fae, but the small fairies around Rita hovered over her, shielding her from further attack.

I looked over at Lilly. Confusion filled her eyes and my mother's necklace at her breast glowed and hummed. Trying to speak, I was pushed away from her by a male Fae dressed in medieval garb. He dragged me ten feet away and stood over me, ready to strike with the same razor sharp claws, when Aaron appeared and pulled him off me, throwing him twenty yards away over the east wall. He glared at me for a second and his dark eyes were suddenly rimmed with blue light and said in a guttural voice, "Guard Lilly, protect her." Then, he turned and ran back to fight.

My attention was suddenly brought back to the battle, as I searched franticly for Lilly. All I could see was fine, powdery dust as thick as fog, and the occasional thrown Fae and sailing Angel. It felt as if I was in a drug induced dream; everything was glowing in surreal colors and light. Then, I spotted her thirty feet to my left, crouching on the ground as a golden light radiated from the necklace, casting a clear path for the angels to see the advancing Fae.

It was obvious the Fae were no match for the angels. Many of their lifeless shells were on the ground; their impish faces were contorted with pain. Angels were everywhere, their golden light piercing everything in their path, advancing toward Morgana. Her beautiful features were clouded by rage and disbelief. Suddenly, she shrieked, loud and shrill, as she raised her arms. Her army instantly stopped fighting and abruptly fell to their knees. "Enough!" she said, spinning around in a circle. "Call them off Rita or I will call the Dark Lord!"

Rita pulled her wings in close to her side and hummed, and the angels stood still. The clearing suddenly grew quiet.

"Morgana, your human sacrifice has been made," Rita said, looking down at the lifeless shells of Fae on the ground … and Matty's lifeless body.

Morgana turned to Rita and shrieked, "What do you know of sacrifice?" she bellowed, as the remaining faye cowered into the shadows. My shoulder was bleeding again. Weak from the loss of blood, I sank to the ground with my eyes trained on Lilly.

Rita shook her wings and they fanned even farther out into the field. "I know that one must be made with an honest heart, like the ones we made eons ago," Rita said.

Morgana laughed, then turned to speak to Aaron, "She speaks to me of sacrifice!"

Aaron looked at the chalice now empty at his feet and the blood soaking into the dampened ground. "Goddess, you never said that Lilly would have to die," Aaron said, coming to his senses. "You just said that she would have to release me."

Lilly fingered the necklace and looked at Aaron. "I release you, Aaron," she said kindly. "Your soul can rest now. You don't need Morgana to take you there. The angels will show you the way."

"Liar!" Morgana yelled. She lunged at Lilly and grabbed at the necklace. "He doesn't want to go to the other side of the moon! He wants to follow it to the other world!" Just as her hands encircled Lilly's throat, Aaron picked up Morgana's dagger and plunged it into her back. Her hands fell limply to her side and she turned to face him. "Why Aaron?" she asked, fading before our eyes as her power grew weak.

We watched as she sank to the ground. Suddenly, a fissure opened up in the ground, creating a pathway to the other world. Rita drew her wings close to her body and stepped next to Lilly. They both looked at Aaron, and he, too, seemed to be fading in the rain. Rita lifted her hand and placed it on Aaron's shoulder.

"It is your choice now. You made your sacrifice," Rita said, looking at him with kind eyes. "You can follow her to the other world or journey with us to the other side of the moon."

Aaron looked at Lilly. From my position on the ground I couldn't see her face, but the silent shaking of her shoulders let me know that she was crying.

"Do you forgive me, Lilly?" Aaron asked sincerely.

"I forgive you, Aaron," Lilly said, stroking the side of his cheek. "Go with Rita."

Aaron looked at Rita, then his gaze fell to Matty. "Can we help him?"

Another angel broke rank from the army behind Rita and walked to Matty. He placed his hands on Matty's empty body and prayed in Latin. "Your kindness for your killer shows your true heart, Aaron," he said. "We will make sure that his soul passes to the other side unhindered. He has paid his debt."

Then, Rita reached out and took Lilly's hand. "Your prayers set the stage for redemption," she said and Aaron reached out and took Rita's other hand. Suddenly, the fissure in the ground closed, sending the remaining faye into it with Morgana. "Your choice has been made then, Aaron. Your soul, too, will now find rest."

"Daemon," Lilly said, turning to face me.

The three turned and walked to me and Rita bent and touched my face. "My nephew, we meet at last. I was with your mother today as she passed to the other side. Her final gift was this necklace to Lilly. Her soul was the second soul needed to clear the path for Aaron. Now she is with Matty, and the circle can be complete to fix Morgana's interference." Suddenly, the tip of her wing touched my wounded shoulder and a brilliant golden light filled the space around us. Then, the pain withdrew from my body in almost tangible waves.

When the light faded, Lilly and I were alone in the clearing. Over the eastern wall we saw the retreating figures of the angels, led by the brilliant golden wings of Aunt Rita. On her left hand side was Aaron, supported by the same wing tip that had healed me.

I looked at Lilly's tear-stained face and buried my head in her lap. We sat like that for an immeasurable amount of time. Then, the sky cleared and stars shone brightly above the tree cover. We looked into each other's eyes and I pushed Lilly's auburn hair back behind her ear. The weary look on her face was also one of peace.

"How did you get the necklace?" I asked, breaking the silence.

She held it in her hand once again, fingering the delicate knot. It was a one of a kind piece, as far as I knew. "When I walked into the clearing something caught my eye on the grass. I bent down and it was the necklace. I had seen it before in one of my dreams. I dreamed of your mother before I even met her. In my dream, she sat, fingering this necklace. There were two small boys in the room, you and Matty. I know that now." She said, stopping to look into my eyes. "I knew that I had the dream for a reason, so when I saw the necklace laying in the clearing, I picked it up."

I stroked her cheek, looking into her mesmerizing green eyes. "I saw you stop, but then you pressed your hands to your cheeks," I said. "I had no idea what you were doing."

She laughed, then said, "I thought that I'd better hide it. Did Rita say that your mom …"

"Yes," I replied, nodding my head. "That must be why Aaron's trick with the dagger worked."

Lilly pulled me into her arms. "I'm so sorry, Daemon."

We both looked at the lifeless form of Matty on the ground. "I think that he finally atoned for his sins, but did he have to shoot me?"

Lilly shook her head in disbelief. "Daemon, there's so much that I don't understand."

I took both her hands in mine and pulled her up. "I don't think we're supposed to understand. It might be beyond our comprehension," I said, flexing my shoulder. Not even a scar remained, even though my shirt was torn and bloody. We walked hand in hand to the gate to retrieve our backpacks. I picked my gun up from the ground and tucked it into the waistband of my pants.

Lilly stopped me as I walked over to the gates. "I want to take care of Matty. We can't leave him here like this," she said.

I nodded silently and walked over to his body. Finally, in death, he was free from his demons. Without ceremony, we buried him in a simple grave over the eastern wall.

Becca Boucher

Epilogue

Lilly

Six months after the Eve of Samhain, I finally let myself sit and reflect on everything that had happened. Life had returned to normal. In fact, it was better than we could have hoped for. Daemon and I eloped in the Berkshires on Christmas Eve with Kevin standing by our sides. Our left hands were now adorned with matching silver Claddagh rings. We returned home to find an acceptance letter to med school for Daemon, and we soon settled into a simple routine of school and work.

I took the job as director of nutrition at the local day health program and loved every second of working again. We had contacted the trusties of the Quaker Cemetery and received permission to have Daemon's mother buried there, although we never told anyone about Matty. The police had relegated his file to the cold case pile and we received updates every now and then that "no news was good news." Everyone assumed that he had left the country.

Some time later, we found ourselves hiking through the wet woods early in spring, retracing the now familiar path to the cemetery. Mary's grave lay on the side of the east wall that was the cemetery proper, not far from where we had buried Matty. The sun was warm through the trees as I planted the pink and white peonies that I had brought along. The necklace of the virgin and child lay in its permanent place around my neck, between my breasts. I watched as Daemon climbed back over the wall and walked toward me.

"I still think we should have planted lilies," he said with a smile. "She would have gotten a kick out of that."

I laughed as I stood and brushed the dirt off my pants. "Next time," I said, then asked, "Is everything all right over there?"

He glanced back over his shoulder at the cemetery and said, "Yeah. Everything is fine. I covered the marker back over with moss. Someday, enough time will have passed that we won't have to hide it."

A little shiver passed over me as I looked at the knoll. "I'm glad not too many people remember that this is here. It's really kind of pretty," I asked, feeling that this was our place. I took a deep breath and asked, "You ready to go?"

Daemon wrapped his arms around my waist and pressed his lips to my forehead. "Do you still ever wonder what would have happened if fate hadn't stepped in?"

I shook my head. "Aren't you the one who said that maybe we weren't meant to understand?" I asked, laughing.

We started to walk toward the gates. "Yeah, but, if Matty had never snapped and Aaron had gone to Scotland, would I have met you? Would he have been saved from Morgana?" he asked. I slowed my pace to match his, my smile gone. "And Aunt Rita is an angel? You know, sometimes I feel like she is still watching me … guiding me."

I waited as he closed the gate and we turned back down the path to the road. "Daemon, I think about it sometimes, but I think it was in the cards all along. It was fate. Before we can enjoy the good things in life, we have to endure the pain … and if it means keeping you, I would do it all over again."

We walked silently hand in hand until we were in sight of the Camaro again, parked on the main road, but something was nagging at me. I pulled back as Daemon opened the door for me. "There's one thing that bothers me," I said, concerned. "Kat. Try as I may, I have not been able to connect her to this. Why was she so angry?"

Becca Boucher

Daemon placed me in the car with a kiss and walked around to the driver's side. He got in and closed the door, then rested his hands on the steering wheel. "Jealousy … that you had Aaron … anger that in her mind you didn't fully play the role of 'grieving widow'," he said, taking a deep breath. "I guess that's one of the things we aren't meant to understand."

I looked out the window as the engine roared to life and Daemon turned the car toward home. "I guess so," I said, still feeling a bit unsettled … along with the rest of the thoughts left unspoken within my mind.

Author's Note

As with all works of fiction, I put my own spin on Celtic lore and tradition. If you would like to read more on the Celtics and fairies, there are numerous web sites and books that can start you in the right direction.

Daemon and Lilly are characters purely from my imagination, but the world that they inhabit is a mixture of the small town I reside in and other small towns around me, but I feel it important to note that the Quaker Cemetery—or Friend's Cemetery—is a real cemetery ran by the Worcester Society of Friends, the Quakers. It is, in fact, hidden deep in the woods, and is the site for many spooky tales and legends.

I grew up hearing tales of this cemetery and it was ingrained into my memory. All the locals around here know it by its nickname, Spider Gates. (The gates leading into the cemetery are intricately carved to look like spider webs.) It is listed as the most haunted cemetery in Central Massachusetts. I have found it, and it was sitting in a quiet, grassy knoll when the image of Lilly entering the cemetery, being watched by someone in the shadows, was born. When I started writing *Hunting the Moon,* I just knew that I would have to explore further the "haunted" places around me.

Quaker Cemetery is still in use and contains graves dating back to the late 1600's and internments as recent as 2009. I beg anyone with interest in history and old cemeteries to tread lightly on these properties and respect the souls that are buried there.

Becca Boucher

About the Author

Becca Boucher

Becca Boucher was born and raised in Worcester Massachusetts. Her father instilled an early love of reading in her and encouraged her when she started to write. Rebecca earned a degree in Criminal Justice from Quinsigamond Community College, but her love has always been writing. After the birth of her first child, she moved to a quiet little town on the edge of Worcester County, in the heart of Central Massachusetts. Living there has inspired her to write most of her current projects. In fact, local readers might recognize some of her locations.

Currently, Becca is a freelance writer and blogger. Her first novel *is Hunting the Moon (The Moon Series)*. Rebecca is also the Write More Publications blog tour coordinator and an avid Beta reader.

When she is not writing, Becca is the mother of two boys, ages 10 and 13. Her youngest son was diagnosed in the Autism spectrum, and a lot of her volunteer time is spent raising awareness and promoting education for that cause.

Acknowledgements

This book has been a long time coming, and wouldn't have gotten to this point without the encouragement of some really important people. There are always tons of people to thank, so to every one of my family, friends, and Facebook fans, thank you from the bottom of my heart.

First, Jamie Wagner. Girl you are the sister that I always wanted. From the second you caught the bouquet at my wedding you have had my back and have given me a safe place to run. I hope you know how much you mean to me.

Emlyn Chand, you taught me everything that I know about blogging and social media. You gave me a shot in this crazy writing world we inhabit, and encouraged me to follow my dreams. You will always be the bar I strive to reach.

Jamie Sue Wilsoncroft, what can I say? Through an awesome blog lady we met and became close friends. You read the first haphazard copy of *Hunting The Moon* and sent it to Theresa. Without you, no one would be reading this book. You, too, mean the world to me.

My best buds, Molly Bryant and Simone Reed. Girls, when we finally meet in person the world might not be able to handle it. Thank you both for always being there for me.

Theresa, you rock! You made this book shine and I love working with you.

And last but not least, my boys, Chander and Dale. You two are my reason for living and striving for my dreams. How can I teach you to strive for yours if I don't chase mine? God gave me the best gift when he let me be your mom.
Love you to the moon and back.

The following is a preview of:

Midnight Raven
(The Moon Series, Book 2)

Coming soon from:
Write More Publications

"When all you want is to be loved unconditionally and everyone puts conditions on you, you tend to give up on life."

—*Cace Matthews*
Midnight Raven

Chapter 1

Kat

Jogging always made sense to me. It was more than a way to keep my body in shape; it was a way to clear my mind and rid it of clutter. In college, Lilly and I would jog for hours, running side by side in silence. After Aaron was killed, we ran longer and harder. I tried to keep up with Lilly as she ran from her fear. Then, I added to her fear. It occurred to me that night as I ran into the twilight that I hadn't been the friend Lilly needed. Hell, I hadn't been a good wife or mother, either. I was selfish, egotistical, and somewhere along the way I had turned into some bitch I hardly recognized. It took Brad leaving for me to realize that. It took his moving out to make me realize that I married him out of spite. All ever wanted was Aaron, but Aaron loved Lilly.

Then, I threw my jealousy in her face, trampling on his memory, all to make myself feel better. The thought made my eyes tear, so I ran faster, pushing myself until my lungs felt as if they would burst from the exertion. Thinking of how I had behaved always made me want to punish myself. I had let Brad take the kids. I pushed Lilly away. I put up a wall of self-hatred that pushed everyone that I needed from my life … and all I could do was run.

I reached the top of the hill and stopped, resting my hands on my knees and taking deep breaths to fill my lungs and ease the ache, the physical one, at least. The sky was growing dark. Clouds were moving in and the stars were obscured. I knew it was risky to run at night. By the time I ran the three miles back home it would be pitch black, but I didn't care. Part of me knew that I was flirting with danger by running into the night, and part of me craved that danger … a self-imposed penance for the sins of my selfishness.

I ran my fingers through my short, red hair, pushing the sweat band back into place and repositioning the ear buds from my I-pod back into a comfortable position. I stretched my hands over my head and reached behind my back, working all the kinks from my neck. Six miles should be enough for tonight. I could go home and take a hot shower and plan my rounds for tomorrow. Turning, I started back down the hill, when a shadow of wings flew close by my head. My eyes darted up to catch the outline of a raven up against the cold, gray sky. Funny, I had never seen a raven up here before. He turned around and swooped down by the edge of the lake before soaring back into the night sky. Suddenly, a line of long forgotten poetry jumped into my mind, a line from "The Raven," by Edgar Allan Poe.

*"Open here I flung the shutter, when,
with many a flirt and flutter, in there stepped
a stately raven of the saintly days of yore."*

Becca Boucher

Where did that come from? My tenth grade English teacher would love to know that random bits of poetry jumped into my head. I shook the fog from my brain and started the jog home; all thoughts of the bird were forgotten.

Cace

In this form I didn't have to think. My body functioned on instinct, my responses were automatic. I let the current of the wind carry me over town. Banking to the left I flew out over the lake, dipping low to catch the wayward insect, then rising higher to soar through the clouds. My wings spread like a blanket into the night sky. I was free ... free from feeling, from torment, from expectations. Black as the coming night, I could soar for hours until I found the perfect spot to rest. No one to miss me, and there was no one to answer to.

The human part of me that remained was pushed to the back of my conciseness, taking in information that I would later need. Of all the forms I could take, this one was my favorite, my go to. Wasn't it every child's dream to fly, and every adult's, too? I could fly whenever I wanted, leaving the human pain behind.

But tonight wasn't about pain; I had just wanted to fly. I slowed and banked back around to fly over the lake one last time. Coming close to the water, I leaned my slender, black head down to let my beak pick up any scent that might lead me to dinner. She registered on my radar too late. I flew right by her head, picking up on the sweet scent of vanilla from her perfume. She looked up and her eyes took me in. There was no shock or revulsion, just surprise. I was adept at picking up on emotions. I sensed her beauty as I turned and flew back by the water. The human part of my brain committed her to memory as I flew to the top of the tallest tree.

Made in the USA
Charleston, SC
21 January 2014